INSPECTOR WITHERSPOON ALWAYS TRIUMPHS...
HOW DOES HE DO IT?

Even the Inspector himself doesn't know—because his secret weapon is as ladylike as she is clever. She's Mrs. Jeffries—the determined, delightful detective who stars in this unique Victorian mystery series! Be sure to read them all . . .

The Inspector and Mrs. Jeffries
A doctor is found dead in his own office—and Mrs. Jeffries must scour the premises to find the prescription for murder!

Mrs. Jeffries Dusts for Clues
One case is solved and another is opened when the Inspector finds a missing brooch—pinned to a dead woman's gown. But Mrs. Jeffries never cleans a room without dusting under the bed—and never gives up on a case before every loose end is tightly tied . . .

The Ghost and Mrs. Jeffries
Death is unpredictable but the murder of Mrs. Hodges was foreseen at a spooky seance. The practical-minded housekeeper may not be able to see the future—but she can look into the past and put things in order to solve this haunting crime!

Mrs. Jeffries Takes Stock
A businessman has been murdered—and it could be because he cheated his stockholders. The housekeeper's interest is piqued—and when it comes to catching killers, the smart money's on Mrs. Jeffries!

Mrs. Jeffries On the Ball
A festive Jubilee celebration turns into a fatal affair—and Mrs. Jeffries must find the guilty party . . .

Mrs. Jeffries On the Trail
Why was Annie Shields out selling flowers so late on a foggy night? And more importantly, who killed her while she was doing it? It's up to Mrs. Jeffries to sniff out the clues . . .

Mrs. Jeffries Plays the Cook
Mrs. Jeffries finds herself doing double duty: cooking for the Inspector's household and trying to cook a killer's goose . . .

Mrs. Jeffries and the Missing Alibi
When Inspector Witherspoon becomes the main suspect in a murder, Scotland Yard refuses to let him investigate. But no one said anything about Mrs. Jeffries . . .

MRS. JEFFRIES
STANDS CORRECTED

EMILY BRIGHTWELL

BERKLEY PRIME CRIME, NEW YORK

MRS. JEFFRIES STANDS CORRECTED

A Berkley Prime Crime Book / published by arrangement with the author

PRINTING HISTORY
Berkley Prime Crime edition / December 1996

All rights reserved.
Copyright © 1996 by The Berkley Publishing Group.
This book may not be reproduced in whole or in part,
by mimeograph or any other means, without permission.
For information address: The Berkley Publishing Group,
200 Madison Avenue, New York, NY 10016.

The Putnam Berkley World Wide Web site address is
http://www.berkley.com/berkley

ISBN: 0-425-15580-3

Berkley Prime Crime Books are published
by The Berkley Publishing Group,
200 Madison Avenue, New York, NY 10016.
The name BERKLEY PRIME CRIME and the BERKLEY PRIME CRIME
design are trademarks belonging to Berkley Publishing Corporation.

PRINTED IN THE UNITED STATES OF AMERICA

10 9 8 7 6 5 4 3 2 1

To Matthew James Arguile
My own special gift from God

CHAPTER 1

"So you can see, gentlemen," Haydon Dapeers said to the two men standing on the other side of the polished mahogany bar, "I've done myself proud. The Gilded Lily Pub is a showplace. Take a look at the etched-glass windows." He gestured toward the front of the pub. "You won't see the likes of those very often. I hired an artist, mind you, not some glass cutter, to do that work. And what about the partitions—solid wood, they are. Cost me almost as much as those fancy brass gas lamps and fittings. Not that I'm complaining about the expense; you've got to spend money to make money. That's what I always say. And I say it's money well spent. I'll have customers fighting to get in here."

Edward Magil glanced at his companion, Luther Pump. "The pub certainly is beautiful, Mr. Dapeers," Magil agreed, "but we didn't come to inspect your premises. That's hardly our concern. We came to speak with you about that other matter. The one you wrote us about today.''

''A matter of some importance,'' Luther Pump added. He glanced around the rapidly filling public bar. Dapeers might be a bit of a braggart, but the man did have a point. The pub was beautiful. The lingering rays of the June sunshine sparkled through the large windowpanes at the front. Huge lilies, etched within fantastical curved lines, cast intricate patterns against the dark oak floor. Brass lamplights, their bases shaped like lily stems, decorated the richly papered walls. Potted ferns had been placed strategically around the room and the partitions between the public and saloon bars were dark wood panels polished to a high gloss.

''You've picked a bad day, gentlemen.'' Haydon pursed his thin lips. ''I don't really have time to talk with you now. People are starting to come in. It's my birthday and our opening night. I do wish you'd come around earlier this afternoon. I could have spared a few moments for you then.''

''A few moments?'' Pump raised one dark eyebrow and picked a piece of lint off the cuff of his immaculate black suit. ''Mr. Dapeers, may I remind you that you wrote to us.''

''Of course I did,'' Haydon agreed apologetically. ''But I didn't expect you to come so quickly.''

''Of course we came straightaway,'' Magil said. ''You've made a very serious charge.''

''I'll grant that the matter is important.'' Haydon gave the ever-increasing crowd a worried frown. ''But can't it wait until tomorrow?''

Magil's lips pursed in disapproval. ''Mr. Dapeers, we're very busy. . . .''

''The bottom tap is stuck, Mr. Dapeers,'' Molly, the barmaid, yelled from the far end of the bar. ''I can't serve beer if this ruddy things goin' to be actin' up all evening."

Haydon Dapeers rolled his eyes. "Just a minute, Molly."

Luther Pump sighed and looked at his companion. "It's no use, Edward. We might as well make an appointment for Mr. Dapeers to come see us tomorrow. One more day isn't going to hurt." He turned back to the publican. "We'll expect you in our offices first thing tomorrow morning. This is a very serious charge you've made. Very serious indeed."

"I appreciate your understanding," Haydon said pompously. "Molly," he called, "get these gentlemen some beer. It's on the house." He nodded to the two men and started toward the other end of the bar, determined to get that stubborn tap to work properly. But his attention was caught by the couple coming in the front door. It was his brother, Tom, and his wife, Joanne.

Haydon smiled maliciously as he watched them take their first look at the Gilded Lily Pub. People always said that Tom Dapeers was a younger version of himself, not that Haydon could see the resemblance. All he saw was a thin little fellow with a long, bony face, mousy-brown hair and pale hazel eyes. Joanne, on the other hand, was a handsome woman. Black-haired, blue-eyed and with an hourglass figure that could turn heads . . . until she opened her mouth. She had the tongue of a shrew, the carriage of a queen and more clothes than the Princess of Wales. Haydon sneered slightly as he took in her attire. The cow was tarted up like she was visiting the palace! Her dark red silk dress was festooned with lace at the throat and wrists, the double skirt was layered in rosettes and she even carried a matching muff and parasol. Ye gods, Haydon thought, it would be a cold day in hell before he'd ever let Moira make a spectacle of herself like that. But tonight he didn't have to bother with insulting his sister-in-law's clothes. All he had to do was stand back and watch her turn green with envy.

"Come in, come in," Haydon called, waving to the new-comers. "I wondered if you two would come and get a gander at the competition." He'd known good and well that wild horses couldn't have kept his sister-in-law away.

"Of course we came, Haydon," Tom Dapeers replied.

Joanne's lips curled slightly. "A bit too much brass for my taste," she said, turning in a slow circle to take in every detail of the room. "But I suppose there's some that will like it. Nice. But it doesn't hold a candle to any of our pubs."

Haydon Dapeers came out from behind the bar and walked over to them, leaving Magil and Pump to enjoy their drink. "I think there's going to be lots that like it, little brother," he said, totally ignoring his sister-in-law. "And what's more, I think they'll like it enough to leave the two of you wondering where all your trade's gone. You won't have to look far, now, will you?"

"Mr. Dapeers," Mick, the barman, called, "the other tap's stuck now. Can you come and give us a hand?"

"In a minute, Mick, in a minute."

"Having trouble, Haydon?" Joanne Dapeers asked. She smiled spitefully.

"Not a bit, just a couple of sticky taps. I'll get them fixed straightaway." Haydon nodded toward the two men in suits at the bar. "Place is filling up nicely; even have a couple of guests from Bestal's Brewery."

"Expect they're wantin' to see if you're wasting their money or not," Joanne replied shortly. "Come on, Tom, let's get a beer before the crowd gets too thick." She tugged her husband's arm and they wandered to the bar.

The Gilded Lily continued to fill up. Within half an hour Haydon's wife, Moira, his other sister-in-law Sarah Hewett and numerous other friends and acquaintances had come by. Haydon was kept busy darting from one group to another, refilling glasses and seeing to his guests' comfort.

He didn't notice a tall young man with light brown hair and deep-set hazel eyes come in. It was only as he was looking around the room, trying to see if the men from Bestals were still there, that he saw him.

Haydon rushed over to the corner where the man and Sarah Hewett were standing close together. "What are you doing here, Taggert?" he demanded, glaring at the young man.

"This is a public house," Sarah said quickly. She was a lovely young woman of twenty-three with dark blond hair, gray eyes and a full sensual mouth. "He's as much right to be here as anyone."

"Let me handle this." Michael Taggert put his hand on Sarah's arm. "I came by for my money," he said to Dapeers. "You still owe me for the windows and the carving on the bar. I want to be paid."

"I'm not givin' you a ruddy farthing till I'm good and ready," Haydon snapped. "And I'll thank you to stay away from Sarah."

"I can see who I like," Sarah hissed.

"Not while you and your brat are living in my house, you can't."

"She'll not be living there much longer," Taggert warned, "and you'd best keep your bloody hands to yourself. If I hear you've tried to touch her again . . ."

"I don't know what you're talking about," Haydon blustered, but he glanced around to see who might be lurking nearby, listening.

"Michael, please," Sarah begged. "Don't start anything tonight. I told you, I'll be all right."

"Good advice." Haydon sneered. "Now get out before I throw you out."

Michael Taggert hesitated. He looked as though he wanted to smash his fist into Haydon's face, but the pleading expression in Sarah's eyes stopped him. "I'll leave. But be warned, Dapeers, you leave Sarah alone. And I want my money. Either you pay me, or I'll have you in court."

"You'll get your ruddy money; now get out of here before I have you thrown out."

"Is something wrong, Haydon?" Moira Dapeers asked softly.

Haydon whirled around at the sound of his wife's voice. "No, my dear, everything's just fine."

Moira Dapeers smiled warmly at Taggert. "How nice to see you again, Mr. Taggert," she said. "I'm so glad you could come by."

"Mr. Taggert was just leaving," Haydon said.

"On the contrary." Michael Taggert smiled slowly. "I'm in no rush. I think I'll stay for a while."

"Haydon," Moira asked, "who is that disreputable-looking person over there? He said he was a friend of yours." She pointed to the bar, where a portly, red-haired man in a dirty porkpie hat and a brown checkered waistcoat was wiping his nose on his sleeve.

Haydon grimaced. "He's not a friend, exactly," he said quickly. "But I better go and have a word with him." Nodding brusquely at his wife, he stalked over to the bar. "What the blazes are you doing here?" he whispered, hoping his wife hadn't taken it into her head to follow him.

"Now, now." Blimpey Groggins finished wiping his nose. "Is that any way to speak to a customer?"

"Customer," Haydon hissed. He glanced behind him and saw that Moira was still talking to Taggert and Sarah. "This is hardly your sort of place, is it?"

"Wouldn't be caught dead 'ere, if you want to know the truth," Blimpey said amiably. "The beer tastes like cat's piss and all these bloody plants makes me nose run.''

"There's nothing wrong with my beer," Haydon said defensively. "But leaving that aside, what are you doing here?"

Blimpey put his glass down on the polished bartop. "I think you know the answer to that one, mate. I'm givin' you a report. I took care of that little message you wanted delivered."

"For God's sake, did you have to come by tonight to tell me that?" Haydon interrupted. "You could've come round tomorrow."

"Look, mate. I don't much like threatenin' people. I done what you wanted done so's I could get it outta the way, like. Now just give me me lolly and I'll clear off." Blimpey Groggins didn't much like doing this kind of work. Fact was, he hated it. But he hated going hungry more.

Haydon looked around to see if anyone was looking at them. But no one was paying attention. "What did he say?"

Blimpey shrugged. "What they always say. That 'e' needs more time."

"That's all?"

" 'Ey, mate. I didn't stand and chat with the bloke, I just delivered the bleedin' message like you wanted. Now pay me and I'll be on me way."

"I can't pay you right now," Haydon cried. "I've got a roomful of guests."

"You got a cash box full of lolly too," Blimpey pointed out. "And I don't want to 'ave to make another trip round 'ere. I'm a busy man."

"You'll have to come back tomorrow," Haydon insisted. "It's not convenient just now."

Blimpey's eyes narrowed. "Listen, mate, I done me job

and I want me money. Now pay up right now or I'll be
'avin' a little chat with that constable up on the corner.
Understand?''

Haydon glared at him, but Blimpey didn't so much as
blink. ''Oh, all right.'' Again, he looked around to make
sure that no one was watching, then he shoved his hands
in his pocket and drew out a wad of bills. Handing them
to Blimpey, he said, ''Here, now clear out.''

''Fine by me, mate.'' Blimpey pocketed the cash. ''I
don't see why you don't like payin' what you owe. I
thought you was rich? You've got two other pubs beside
this one and your wife's got money. But, blimey, you're
about the stingiest sod I've ever met. Next time you need
a body to do your dirty work, call someone else.'' He shook
his head in disgust, turned and walked out.

Haydon closed his eyes for a moment. When he opened
them a moment later, his expression hardened as he saw
Michael Taggert bending close to Sarah, his lips inches
from her ear as he talked to her.

''Mr. Dapeers, we need another keg.'' Molly's nasal
screech reached him over the noise of the crowd.

Haydon sighed. He was the only one with the key to the
taproom. ''I'll get one, Molly,'' he called, pulling the key
out of his pocket and heading to the small door at the far
end of the bar.

As he stepped into the dimly lighted hallway, Haydon
thought he heard a muffled shout over the din from the
public bar. He stopped, wondering if there had been an
accident or a brawl out on the street. Then he told himself
to mind his own business, he had troubles of his own. He
continued on, past the unused kitchen on one side of the
passageway and the entrance to the saloon bar on the other.
The door to the box room was open as he passed. Haydon
reached over and yanked it shut. At the far end of

the hall, he came to the taproom, unlocked it and stepped inside. He struck a match and lit the gas lamp. He'd just started toward the stack of kegs when the light dimmed, sputtered and then failed completely.

"Bloody hell," he muttered, "what's wrong with that ruddy lamp?" He started to turn when he felt a crushing blow to the side of his head.

The blow stunned him so badly, he didn't even feel the knife slide into his back.

Mrs. Jeffries, housekeeper to Inspector Gerald Witherspoon of Scotland Yard, reached up and tugged at the collar of her brown bombazine dress. Loosening it a bit, she sighed in satisfaction and continued down the back stairs to the kitchen.

The rest of the household, save for the inspector, who was working late this evening, were already sitting around the kitchen table waiting for her. "I'm sorry to be late," she said, "but it took longer at Luty's than I'd planned."

"They left, then?" Smythe, the coachman, asked. He was a big man with dark hair, harsh features and a pair of rich brown eyes that generally sparkled with good humor.

"Oh yes, I saw them off." Mrs. Jeffries pulled out a chair at the head of the table and sat down.

"How long are they going to be gone?" Betsy, the maid, asked. She brushed a stray lock of blond hair off her cheek. She was a pretty young woman of twenty, with bright blue eyes, a slender figure and an inquisitive nature.

"I believe Luty and Hatchet were still having words over that very issue when I left," Mrs. Jeffries replied with a smile. The housekeeper was a handsome middle-aged woman in her fifties, with dark auburn hair streaked with gray at the temples, a plump motherly figure and a pair of smiling brown eyes that masked a keen intelligence.

"Typical," Mrs. Goodge, the cook, snorted. "Them two are the only people I know who'd be arguin' over how long they was goin' to stay on holiday just as they were boardin' the train to go."

"Luty is bound and determined to stay for the entire two weeks," Mrs. Jeffries explained, "while Hatchet wants to come back after only one week."

"That's funny," Wiggins, the baby-faced, round-cheeked footman said. "It's usually Hatchet that likes goin' to places like Lord Lovan's country house. What's got into 'im?"

"He hates Scotland," Mrs. Jeffries replied. "Claims the air makes him dizzy."

"Rubbish." The cook reached for the pitcher of light ale and poured herself a glass. "There must be more to it than that. Hatchet's never been dizzy in his life!"

"He's probably scared he'll miss a murder if 'e's gone too long," Smythe suggested. "It's about time for another one; we 'aven't 'ad us a good one since March."

"I don't want another one yet," Wiggins cried. "It's too bloomin' 'ot to be dashing about all over London lookin' for clues and—"

"You never want us to have one," Betsy said accusingly, glaring at the young footman.

"That's not true," Wiggins said defensively. "I just don't like the idea of some poor person gettin' murdered just so's we won't be bored, that's all."

"Smythe wasn't advocating killing anyone." Mrs. Goodge jumped into the argument too. "He was merely saying that Hatchet's only reason for not wanting to stay too long at Lord Lovan's was because he didn't want to chance missing one."

"Really, Wiggins," Mrs. Jeffries said soothingly, "none of us like murders, but the fact is they do happen. Why, none of us came to work for the inspector with any idea that we'd end up investigating his cases."

She was referring to the fact that Inspector Gerald Witherspoon, formerly a clerk in the records room, was now, thanks considerably to their efforts, Scotland Yard's leading investigator of homicides. The fact that no one, including the inspector, could account for his phenomenal success, was also their doing.

"What's the matter," Betsy asked, "don't you like investigating?"

"'Corse I like it." Wiggins frowned. "It's just that I don't want to 'ave one now, that's all. It's too bloomin' 'ot."

"You just don't want anything comin' up and takin' you away from Maureen," Smythe teased. "Mind you, I don't blame ya, lad, she's a fine-lookin' girl."

"Maureen's got nuthin' to do with it," Wiggins protested, but his round apple cheeks turned bright red and he couldn't quite look the coachman in the eye.

Mrs. Jeffries decided that debating murder and talking about their friends Luty and her butler, Hatchet, were one thing. Teasing poor Wiggins about his romantic endeavors was something else. "Well," she said firmly, "I don't think it's up to any of us when a murder will happen. Generally, those decisions are made by someone else."

"I'd think you'd be chompin' at the bit for another one," Smythe said, taking a long sip of his ale. "You missed the last one."

"He didn't really miss it," Betsy said. "He only had a broken leg."

"That's right," Mrs. Goodge put in, "and he did his fair share even then."

Mrs. Jeffries beamed approvingly as she saw the footman's blush fade and a pleased grin cross his face. The household was learning. A smile and a few words of praise went a long way to taking the sting out of a bit of teasing.

"And a fine job 'e did too," Smythe added.

"Well, I didn't do all that much," Wiggins said modestly. "And it's not that I don't like snoopin' about and askin' questions; me and Fred enjoy gettin' out and helpin'. It's just that sometimes I get this awful feelin' that we're . . ." He paused, his face creased in concentration.

"We're what?" Mrs. Jeffries prompted. She was genuinely curious now. Wiggins was no fool, something was bothering him, something important.

"I don't know how to put it." The footman shook his head. "But sometimes I almost get the feelin' that we're makin' a murder 'appen just so we can 'ave an excuse to get out and 'unt down the killer."

"Don't be daft," Mrs. Goodge scoffed.

"That's silly," Betsy cried.

"Don't be so stupid, lad," Smythe said.

Mrs. Jeffries frowned at them all. "Just a moment now. Don't be too quick to judge Wiggins's words. His concern is important."

"But, Mrs. Jeffries." Betsy pushed her plate of cheese, bread and pickled onion to one side and leaned forward. "None of us would ever wish death on someone else. Wiggins is just bein' fanciful."

"But if it's bothering him, Betsy," the housekeeper replied calmly, "then I think it's important we bring it out in the open and discuss it." She turned her attention to the footman. "Do you really think that simply because we've proved ourselves to be quite good at solving murder that we're actually causing them to happen?"

Wiggins looked down at the floor and stared at the top of Fred, their mongrel dog's head. "Well, if you put it like that, it does sound silly," he admitted.

"And do you think that if we stopped investigating the inspector's cases, that murder would disappear from the city of London?" she continued.

" 'Corse not," he said. "It's just that sometimes I get this feelin' . . ."

"Feelin'?" Smythe interjected. "What kind of feelin'?"

Wiggins shrugged helplessly. "I'm not sure. But sometimes I feel right bad inside. 'Ere we are, sitting around bein' bored doin' the household chores and all of us wishin' we 'ad a good excuse to get out and about and do a bit of snoopin'. Then the next thing you know, the inspector's got 'imself a case and we're all 'appy as larks and some poor person's dead. It don't feel right, that's all."

Everyone gazed at him silently. The only sound was the ticking of the clock on the wall and the far-off sound of street traffic coming through the open window of the kitchen.

Finally, Mrs. Jeffries said, "Wiggins, I'm sorry you feel that way. Would you rather stay out of the inspector's cases from now on?"

"No," he cried, his eyes widening in alarm. "I didn't mean that. 'Elpin' solve murders is important work, we've done a lot of good in this city—" He broke off and smiled sheepishly. "Oh, toss me for a game of tin soldiers, I don't know what I'm on about tonight. Just leave it go, will ya? Must be this 'eat that's makin' me rattle on. We're not such a bad lot, even if we do get bored every now and again and want us another murder."

"Good," Mrs. Jeffries said firmly. "I was hoping you'd come to that conclusion. I too think we do some very important work."

The fact that the entire household and their friends Luty Belle Crookshank and her butler, Hatchet, frequently helped solve the inspector's murder cases was an important part of their lives. Not that dear Inspector Witherspoon had any idea he was getting help, of course. That would never do.

Gerald Witherspoon had been a clerk in the records room when he'd inherited this house from his late aunt Euphemia. He'd also inherited a modest fortune. Smythe and Wiggins had come with the house; Mrs. Jeffries, Mrs. Goodge and Betsy were later additions. How fortunate, Mrs. Jeffries thought as she surveyed the faces around the table, that all of them were dedicated to the man and to solving murders.

They were really quite good at it.

Inspector Gerald Witherspoon tried not to look directly at the body sprawled on the floor next to an unopened keg of beer. He didn't much care for corpses. Especially the ones that still had knives sticking out of their backs.

"Doesn't look like he's been dead long, sir," Constable Barnes said. "The body's still warm."

Witherspoon suppressed a shudder.

"Mind you, the heat could account for the body temperature," Barnes said casually, getting to his feet and brushing his hands off. His craggy face creased in worry. "How long ago was he found?"

"Only moments after the murder occurred," Witherspoon murmured. He hoped that Barnes wasn't waiting for him to examine the body; he wasn't sure if he could. He felt rather faint. Must be the heat, he told himself.

"Don't you want to have a look, sir?" Barnes asked, stepping back respectfully.

"Oh no," Witherspoon said quickly. "We'd best wait for the police surgeon. I wouldn't want to destroy any evidence."

As there was nothing but a dead man with a knife stuck

between his shoulder blades, the constable didn't see how the inspector having a look at the body would destroy anything. But he wasn't one to question his superior's motives. Barnes reached up and pulled off his helmet; he ran his fingers through his thick, iron-gray hair and sighed. "At least this one didn't lay here all night. In this heat, he'd have been stinkin' to high heaven by tomorrow morning."

Witherspoon's stomach contracted at Constable Barnes's colorful image. He was rather squeamish about such things and it was getting dreadfully difficult to hide the fact that dead bodies and blood and awful things like that made him feel light-headed. It wasn't that he wasn't dedicated to his work, he most certainly was, no one could ever accuse Gerald Witherspoon of neglecting his duty. He just wished that he wasn't expected to stare at the corpses. Gracious, it wasn't as if the knife in the fellow's back was going to tell him anything. "Who discovered the body?"

"The victim's sister-in-law, Joanne Dapeers," Barnes replied, popping his helmet back on his head. "Soon as she saw the body, she started screamin' to high heaven. Luckily, the barman, when he saw what had happened, had the good sense to lock the door and then send for the constable."

"What's the victim's name?"

"Haydon Dapeers. He owned the pub."

"Were there any witnesses?" Witherspoon didn't know why he bothered to ask. He knew there wouldn't be any. There never were witnesses in the cases to which he got assigned. Somehow, that didn't seem to be fair.

"I don't think so, sir," Barnes said.

"But there's a roomful of people out there." Witherspoon gestured toward the public bar with his thumb. "Surely one of them saw something?"

Barnes shook his head. "I don't think so, sir. According

to what Constable Maxton said, everyone was outside or at the window, watching a brawl that broke out on the street when the murder must have happened. That's one of the reasons we got here so quickly. Maxton had come down to stop the fisticuffs. Of course, as soon as he'd arrived the brawlers took off. He'd just started back to his post when the barman comes dashing out and says that someone's been murdered.''

"Oh dear," Witherspoon muttered. He took one last look at the corpse and sighed. This wasn't going to be an easy case, he could feel it in his bones.

From outside the closed door, he heard the sound of heavy footsteps and then a sharp knock. "That's probably the police surgeon," Witherspoon said.

Barnes opened the door and a young red-haired man wearing a dark suit and carrying a medical bag stepped inside. "Good evening, Inspector Witherspoon," the man said pleasantly.

"Good evening," the inspector replied. He stared at the man in confusion. "Where's Dr. Potter?"

"Gout," the fellow replied. He stepped over and knelt down by the body. "Poor Dr. Potter's got a ripping bad case of it; he'll be flat on his back for weeks."

Witherspoon couldn't believe his luck. Potter wasn't his favorite of police surgeons. "Oh dear, how awful for Potter."

"I expect he'll be fit as a fiddle before too long, Inspector." He popped open his bag and began rummaging around inside. "Now, let's see what we have here."

"Do I know you, sir?" Witherspoon asked. The man looked awfully familiar, but the inspector couldn't quite put his finger on where they'd met.

"We met some time ago at St. Thomas's. The name's Bosworth. Dr. Bosworth."

* * *

"This must be most upsetting for you, Mrs. Dapeers," the inspector said kindly, "most upsetting, indeed. I'm so sorry to have to bother you with questions at a time like this, but it's rather important we start looking for whoever did this foul deed immediately."

Moira Dapeers was obviously in shock. A small middle-aged woman, she had brown hair and a thin, rather mournful face. As she sat back against the bright red velvet cushions of the plush seat, her complexion was as white as a ghost. They'd taken her into the privacy of one of the partitioned sections of the public bar, but even a glass of strong Irish whisky hadn't brought the color back to her pale cheeks. "I understand," she said slowly. Her brown eyes were glazed and her lips trembled.

She brushed a lock of hair off her face. "Please, go ahead. I'd like to get this over with so I can go home."

Witherspoon nodded. "When was the last time you saw your husband alive?"

"It must have been around half-past six," she murmured. "Yes, I know it was then, because it was right before the brawl started. Haydon had just gone into the taproom when I heard this awful ruckus from outside."

"And what happened then?"

Moira Dapeers shrugged. "What do you think happened? Everyone went over to the windows to see what was going on in the street."

"Who do you mean by 'everyone'?" Witherspoon asked curiously.

"I mean everyone who was here tonight for Haydon's birthday celebration." Moira's voice trembled as she said her late husband's name. "We had our friends and neighbors round to help us celebrate, you see. It was Haydon's birthday today and we were opening the pub. It was supposed to be a wonderful night, but—'' She broke off and began weeping.

Witherspoon looked at Constable Barnes. ''I think you'd better arrange for one of the constables to take Mrs. Dapeers home. She's in no condition to make a statement right now.''

''Right, sir,'' Barnes said, turning toward the door that led to the public bar. They'd asked the other guests to wait there under the watchful eyes of several constables.

''I'm all right.'' Moira hiccuped softly and brushed the tears off her cheeks. ''Really, I am.''

Witherspoon let his instincts as a gentleman overcome his training as a policeman. ''No, ma'am,'' he said softly, ''you're not. We'll have someone take you home so you can get a good night's rest. Tomorrow we'll come round to take your statement.''

As soon as Moira Dapeers had been escorted out, Witherspoon spoke to Barnes. ''Have the police constables take the statements of everyone who was here tonight. Make sure they get proper names and addresses. Then tell everyone they can go home.''

Barnes stared at him in shock. ''Go home, sir? Without us talking to them?''

''That's right, Barnes.'' He sighed. ''We can start asking questions in the morning. I don't think our killer is likely to bolt tonight.''

''How do you figure that, sir?''

''Because it's obviously one of them and they think they've gotten away with it.'' Witherspoon couldn't put his finger on how he knew this, but he did know it. For once, he was going to do as his housekeeper, Mrs. Jeffries, advised; he was going to rely on his instincts. ''For the moment that's precisely what I want that person to think too. Once everyone's gone, I think I'd better have another word with the police surgeon. He looks like a bright sort of chap.''

Dr. Bosworth nodded at the men with the stretcher and stepped away from the body. "Now, what did you want to ask me, Inspector?"

"What can you tell us about the victim?" Witherspoon asked.

"Well, he died instantly," Bosworth said slowly. "The killer was either an expert on human anatomy or very lucky. The blade sliced clean into the heart, killing the victim within seconds. The heart is a pump, you see." Bosworth's voice rose enthusiastically. "Quite a wonder of nature, actually. People don't really appreciate how very efficient and marvelous an organ it is. Of course, once it stops pumping they learn soon enough. I expect the blade of the weapon lopped off the left ventricle when the knife went into the poor man. Mind you, I won't know for certain till I do the postmortem."

Witherspoon's stomach turned over. "Er, are you certain it was the knife that killed him?"

"There was no evidence of prior poisoning nor any evidence of other bodily injuries except for the blow on the head. But that shouldn't have killed him; it wasn't even hard enough to make a dent in the skull," Bosworth replied. "But again, I won't know for sure until after the postmortem. I'll be doing that tonight, so I should have a report ready for you by tomorrow morning."

"Are you thinking something else killed the man?" Barnes asked the inspector.

"It's always possible, Barnes," Witherspoon replied. "Dr. Bosworth, did you . . . er . . . retrieve the weapon?"

"Naturally." Bosworth pulled a long flat object wrapped in brown paper out of his bag and handed it to Barnes.

"We can't have some poor soul being carted all over London with a knife sticking out of his back, can we? Here's your evidence, all nice and neatly wrapped for you."

"What kind of knife was it?" Witherspoon asked. He took the proffered object and quickly handed it to the constable. He was embarrassed to remember he'd not taken a proper look at it when he'd first come in tonight. But drat, he really hated examining things sticking out of people's backs.

Bosworth snapped his bag closed. "It looks like a common kitchen knife. Not a new one, mind you. The wood handle was worn quite badly. The blade is ten inches long and quite sharp. My guess is it was sharpened very recently."

"You say the handle was worn?" Witherspoon said hopefully. "Then perhaps someone will be able to identify the weapon."

Bosworth shook his head. "When I said it was worn, I didn't mean it had any distinguishing features, Inspector. I meant that it had been washed many times and a bit of the color had washed out of the wood. It's a common kitchen knife. There's nothing extraordinary about the weapon. You can probably find one in every household in London."

CHAPTER 2

"Good evening, sir," Mrs. Jeffries said to the inspector as she took his hat. "You're rather late tonight. We were starting to worry."

"I'm afraid my tardiness couldn't be helped, Mrs. Jeffries. I hope the staff didn't wait dinner on me," Witherspoon replied. "I'm really not in the least hungry."

"It's only a cold supper, sir," Mrs. Jeffries said. "Betsy can bring it up on a tray when you're ready for it. Would you like a glass of sherry before you eat?"

"That's an excellent idea." Witherspoon followed his housekeeper into the drawing room and sat down in his favorite chair. "There's been a murder, you see. Poor chap got himself stabbed tonight. That's why I'm so late getting home."

Mrs. Jeffries deliberately kept her face bland as she handed her employer a glass of pale amber sherry. Wiggins's words tweaked her conscience a bit, but the truth was, she was overjoyed. A murder. They had themselves a murder to investigate.

"How very unfortunate," she said, taking a seat opposite the inspector. "Was it a domestic dispute of some kind?"

She sincerely hoped it wasn't. Those kind of murders were never very interesting to snoop about in; they were simply too obvious. It was almost always a drunken husband or a mousy wife who had been pushed just that bit too hard.

"Oh no, not so far as we can tell." Witherspoon took a sip of sherry. "A publican named Haydon Dapeers was killed. The knife went clean through his heart; at least that's what Dr. Bosworth told me. Can you believe it? The poor man got murdered at his own birthday celebration."

"How awful," Mrs. Jeffries replied. She couldn't believe her good luck. Dr. Bosworth was on the scene! The good doctor had given her information on the inspector's cases on more than one occasion in the past. He was intelligent, observant and most important, he could keep his own counsel. She made a mental note to nip out and see Bosworth first thing tomorrow morning. But for now, she wanted as much information as possible. "Were there any witnesses?"

"No, Dapeers had gone back to the taproom when he was killed. No one saw anything. There was some kind of altercation out on the street when the murder happened. Everyone else in the place had dashed over to the windows or gone outside to have a look."

"Were there a lot of people in the pub when the murder took place?" she asked.

"Actually, it was quite crowded. It was the pub's opening night as well as Haydon Dapeers's birthday. Sad really. Here the man was surrounded by friends and relatives and he ends up getting murdered. I don't know, Mrs. Jeffries''—Witherspoon shook his head sadly—''sometimes I wonder what the world is coming to.''

''Well, sir,'' she said calmly, ''I don't really think I agree with you. Remember, you do see the results of violence more than most people. But do keep in mind that fifty years ago or so, there wouldn't have been someone like you to even investigate this unfortunate person's death. Scotland Yard and the entire police force didn't even exist. At least now our society tries to make sure that justice is done, and you, sir, do more than anyone I know to ensure that it is.'' She decided her dear inspector needed a bit of bucking up. Occasionally, he allowed the more sordid aspects of his work to undermine his self-confidence. She was sure that was what the problem was tonight. He was merely feeling as though he wouldn't be up to the task in front of him.

''How good of you to remind me, Mrs. Jeffries.'' Witherspoon sighed dramatically. ''You're right, of course. I daresay the world hasn't really changed.''

''Actually, sir, I do believe that because of people like yourself, it's a considerably better world than it used to be.'' It never hurt to bolster the man's opinion of himself.

''Thank you. I needed to hear those words.''

''It's a wonder you got home before midnight,'' Mrs. Jeffries said brightly. Now that the inspector was over his obligatory maudlin philosophizing, she wanted to get the details of the murder out of him while they were fresh in his mind. ''What with all those people to interview.''

''Oh, I didn't bother with that,'' Witherspoon replied airily. ''I told Barnes to make sure we had everyone's name and address. I'll start the interviewing tomorrow.''

Shocked, Mrs. Jeffries stared at him. ''You don't think one of the guests is the killer?''

''I've no idea who the killer is.'' He shrugged. ''But my

instinct was to let everyone go home. I thought perhaps it would be best to let the murderer think he'd gotten away with it.'' He smiled kindly at his housekeeper. ''Ever since you told me about listening to my 'inner voice' that time— you must remember, it was when I was having such a difficult time cracking that case. . . .'' He paused, his forehead crinkled in concentration as he tried to recall precisely which case it was. ''Oh, I don't remember exactly which one it was, but it was last year sometime. I was having a dreadful time, simply dreadful. You advised me to listen to my instincts, to let my 'policeman's voice' guide my actions and thoughts. Of course, you were absolutely right and I cracked that case in no time. I'm going to do the same thing on this one.''

Utterly speechless, Mrs. Jeffries gaped at him. Gracious, who would have thought he'd taken her words so seriously? All she'd ever done was to try to make him feel confident about himself. What had she created? ''I see. And you thought it best to let all your suspects leave and go home tonight, is that it?''

''Yes.'' He beamed at her. ''That's it precisely. I saw no point in keeping everyone hanging about the Gilded Lily Pub while I asked questions. I've found that murderers are far more likely to make mistakes when they think they have gotten away with it.''

Mrs. Jeffries didn't agree. But she could hardly say so. Especially as the inspector seemed to be basing his behavior in this case on advice she'd previously given him. ''Exactly where is the Gilded Lily Pub?''

''It's not far from Scotland Yard.'' Witherspoon drained his glass. ''Quite a lovely place, actually. Brass fittings and gilded mirrors, beautiful etched windows and carved panels on the partitions. It's the sort of place where one would feel comfortable taking a lady, if you know what I mean.

Perhaps when Lady Cannonberry returns from the country, we'll try finding an equally refined pub around our own neighborhood here.''

"That's a lovely idea. And the Gilded Lily is close to Scotland Yard, you say?''

"Not far at all.'' He stood up abruptly. "I say, we haven't gotten another letter from Lady Cannonberry, have we?''

"No, sir,'' Mrs. Jeffries forced herself to say calmly. She knew he missed their neighbor, but right now she didn't want to discuss the inspector's romantic affiliations. She wanted facts about this murder. "What time did the murder occur?''

"I think I'll have that cold supper now,'' Witherspoon said just as she asked her question. "I'm suddenly famished.''

"Is that all you got out of 'im?'' Smythe asked incredulously. "Just the name of the pub and the name of the victim?''

Mrs. Jeffries nodded. She felt rather foolish. As soon as the inspector was safely ensconced in the dining room with his supper, she'd called the rest of the household together to tell them the news. But she had so very little to report. "I know it isn't much, but he was in the strangest mood tonight. He wanted to talk about the murder, but he didn't want to say very much.''

"You say he had a room full of suspects and he let them all go home without even interviewing them?'' Mrs. Goodge asked curiously. "That don't sound right.''

"It isn't right,'' Mrs. Jeffries replied. "For some strange reason, the inspector seems to think it's best to let the killer think he got away with it. He won't start interviewing the people who were in the pub when the murder occurred until tomorrow.''

''Did you get us a few of their names?'' Betsy asked hopefully.

''I'm afraid not.''

''Where's this pub at, then?'' Wiggins pressed.

''I'm not really sure,'' Mrs. Jeffries admitted. ''But it's quite near Scotland Yard.''

'' 'Ow about the time of death?'' Smythe stared at her hopefully.

''Sometime this evening.''

''What kinda knife was it?'' Wiggins asked.

''He didn't say.''

''Blimey,'' Smythe exclaimed, ''you didn't get much out of 'im, did ya?''

''It's not Mrs. Jeffries's fault if the inspector has suddenly got tongue-tied,'' Betsy snapped. ''So give it a rest.'' She turned and smiled at the housekeeper. ''What do you think has gotten into him? It's not like the inspector to be so cagey. He usually tells you everything.''

Mrs. Jeffries was at a loss to explain the inspector's behavior to the others. If she told them he was simply acting on advice she'd given him in the past, she'd feel absolutely idiotic. It would be difficult to make them understand. ''He might have just been tired,'' she ventured.

''Me too.'' Wiggins yawned widely. ''I'm dead on me feet. So what do we do now? It's not like we've got much to start on.''

''We've got plenty of information,'' the housekeeper said firmly. Just because Inspector Witherspoon had developed a bad case of discretion didn't mean they weren't going to get started right away. ''We know the name of the victim, the name of the pub, the approximate time of death and we know the killer used a knife.''

"I can find out where this 'ere Gilded Lily Pub is," Smythe volunteered. "If it's near Scotland Yard, I can nip out to the stables tomorrow mornin' and talk to one of the cabbies in the area. They know where all the pubs are."

"But this was a new one," Mrs. Jeffries pointed out. "It had only just opened a few hours before the murder."

Smythe waved a hand dismissively. "That don't matter. The cabbies'll know where it is."

"How quickly can you find out?" Betsy asked.

"Be back before breakfast," he replied, giving the maid a cocky grin. "And then we can get crackin'; right, Mrs. Jeffries?"

Smythe was as good as his word. As they sat down to breakfast the next morning, he rushed in through the back door, paused to pat Fred, who was bouncing at his feet, and then announced that the Gilded Lily Pub was on the corner of Minyard Street and Bonham Road. "It's less than 'alf a mile from Scotland Yard," he finished as he pulled out a chair and sat down.

"So where do we start?" Wiggins asked excitedly.

"I think you should get over to the area and start talking to the street boys and costermongers," Mrs. Jeffries said. "See what you can find out about the victim."

"Do you want me to have a go at the shopkeepers in the area?" Betsy asked.

Mrs. Jeffries regarded her thoughtfully. "No, I want you to find out where Haydon lived and then nip round to his home and see if you can make contact with someone from his household. See what you can find out."

"But he was murdered at the pub," Betsy protested.

"Yes, but Dapeers was at a celebration with his friends and relations," Mrs. Jeffries explained. "So we must find out as much as we can about everyone present and see if any of his relatives or acquaintances had a reason to murder him. The best way to do that is to learn what we can about him and his household. As we all know, it's usually those nearest and dearest to us that are the most dangerous.''

"What about me?'' Mrs. Goodge asked. "I've only got one name to go on, and Dapeers was only a publican. I don't think my sources are goin' to know much about the man.''

Mrs. Jeffries understood the cook's dilemma. Mrs. Goodge had a veritable army of tradespeople who trooped through her kitchen. Costermongers, delivery boys, rag-and-bones men. She also had a wide network of friends from her many years of cooking for the cream of London society. But unfortunately, in this case, Mrs. Goodge was right. It was highly unlikely that any of her sources would know much about a common pub owner. Or would they? "I'm not so sure about that,'' Mrs. Jeffries said. "Perhaps you will find out something. You must try.''

"I don't know, Mrs. Jeffries,'' Mrs. Goodge said sadly. "He's only a pub owner. Not that there's anything wrong with that, but it's not like he had half of London snooping about and watching him when he was alive. Probably no one gave a toss about his coming and goings. It's not like he's anybody important now, is it?''

"Would you like to go out and ask a few questions, then?'' the housekeeper said.

"Certainly not,'' Mrs. Goodge retorted, shocked at the very notion of leaving her kitchen. "I'm staying right here. You just be sure that this lot''—she swept her arm around the table—''gets me some names. My sources may not know anything today about that murder, but they're all just as nosy as we are. A few well-chosen words and I'll have 'em out on the streets learning all sorts of interesting bits and pieces.''

"That's the spirit, Mrs. Goodge." Smythe reached for his tea. "Luty and Hatchet'll both be right narked. You know how Luty 'ates to miss a murder."

"What about Hatchet?" Betsy added. "He's just as bad."

"I wonder if we shouldn't send them a telegram," Mrs. Jeffries murmured. "We could use their help."

"Of course we must send a telegram," Mrs. Goodge agreed. "If Luty misses another murder, we'll never hear the end of it."

The Dapeers house was much grander than Witherspoon expected. The tall, redbrick structure was located on Percy Street, off the Tottenham Court Road. "I must say, he lives in rather a large house for a publican," Witherspoon muttered. He glanced around the elegant drawing room, his gaze noting the pale rose wallpaper, the heavy green velvet curtains at the windows, the intricate wood carving on the top of the mantelpiece and the opulent furnishings. The green-and-rose-striped settee and the contrasting balloon-backed chairs would be worth more than six months of his salary.

"Well," Barnes said softly, "he does own three pubs. But even so, this is a right posh place."

"I think we're in the wrong business," Witherspoon joked.

"Good morning, gentlemen," Moira Dapeers said as she swept into the room. "I'm so sorry to have kept you waiting. Please sit down, gentlemen." She motioned them toward the settee. "That'll be all, Perkins," she said, dismissing the servant.

Witherspoon and Barnes both sat down. Moira Dapeers, wearing a stiff, black bombazine dress, sank down in a chair opposite them. "The household is in a bit of a state

this morning,'' she said, smiling apologetically. "It's not
my habit to keep people waiting. Haydon couldn't stand to
be kept waiting.''

"We're sorry to intrude upon your grief, madam," Witherspoon said formally, "but we've no choice in the matter.
We really must ask you a few questions."

She waved a hand in the air. "Oh, that's all right. Now
that I've gotten over the shock of Haydon's death, I'm quite
able to talk about it."

The inspector studied her thoughtfully. She did, indeed,
appear to have recovered from the shock. Her gaze was
honest and direct, her color excellent, and if he wasn't mis-
taken, she was wearing just the smallest amount of lip
rouge. "Could you please tell us everything that happened
last night?"

"That shouldn't be too difficult," she said brightly. "As
you know, we had the opening of the Gilded Lily scheduled
to coincide with Haydon's birthday. That was his idea, naturally. Personally, I thought it a bit common. Rather like
asking everyone you know to drop in to wish you many
happy returns and then forcing them to hang about and buy
their own drinks.''

"Was the Gilded Lily your husband's only business?"
Constable Barnes asked.

Witherspoon gave him a sharp look, wondering why he
asked a question they already knew the answer to.

"Oh no." She laughed. "We own two other pubs.
They're doing quite well too. Mind you, neither of them is
near as fancy as the Gilded Lily, but they're decent places
and they do us well enough. But Haydon wanted to make
the new pub absolutely spectacular. He poured ever so
much money into it. Brass fittings, velvet benches, etched
windows. Oh my, yes, he was determined to make it a
showplace.''

"Mrs. Dapeers," the inspector said. "About last evening?"

"Oh yes, well, as I was saying, the pub was scheduled to open on Haydon's birthday. He claimed he wanted to make a celebration of it, you see. So he invited some friends and acquaintances to come round. He said he was going to make a bit of a party of the whole thing. But I noticed he didn't give them free beer. Everyone was paying for what they drank."

Witherspoon tried to be patient. He didn't want to have to interrupt a lady, but goodness, how long was she going to harp on her late husband's boorish behavior?

"My sister-in-law and I arrived a little after five o'clock," she continued. "No, that's wrong. We didn't get there until twenty past; it took some time before we were able to get a hansom."

"And who else was there when you arrived?" Witherspoon asked. He'd no idea what he was trying to find out, but he decided to plunge right on in anyway. After all, Mrs. Jeffries was always telling him to trust his "inner voice." Right now that voice was telling him to learn as much as he could and sort it out later. Perhaps he'd oughtn't to be so impatient with the lady. Perhaps if he allowed her to ramble on, she might tell him more than she intended.

"Let me see. . . ." She paused again, her forehead wrinkling in concentration. "There was Molly and Mick, of course. They're our employees. There were one or two other staff members too. Haydon insisted we have a full staff. And I believe he was going to hire another barmaid; I know he was planning on interviewing another one yesterday morning. He was that sure the place would be a success right from opening night and he wanted to make sure we had enough help to take care of our customers."

"Yes, yes," Witherspoon encouraged. "But back to my

question.'' He already had a complete list of who was present when the murder occurred and he wasn't sure why he needed to know who was there before the killing. But something deep inside was telling him it was important information.

Moira cocked her head and stroked her chin as she tried to remember. "The men from Bestal's were there. And Michael Taggert—no,'' she corrected. "I tell a lie; Michael didn't come in until after we'd been there a few minutes. I remember distinctly watching him come through the front door. I was thinking there'd be a ruckus, you see. Haydon was being very mean about Mr. Taggert. He kept finding excuses not to pay the poor boy. I think he was really just being nasty, though.''

"Mr. Taggert and Mr. Dapeers were enemies?'' Witherspoon asked eagerly. He couldn't believe it; Mrs. Jeffries was right. His inner voice was working properly.

"Oh no.'' Moira laughed gaily. "They weren't precisely enemies. But Haydon had hired Mr. Taggert to do the etching on the windows and some intricate wood carving on the back bar. He kept putting off paying him for the work. Mr. Taggert was getting rather insistent, I'm afraid.''

"Was there some kind of altercation between Mr. Taggert and your husband last night?'' Witherspoon began.

"Oh goodness, yes,'' Moira replied cheerfully. "I was rather hoping that Mr. Taggert would take a poke at Haydon. I must say, Haydon would have deserved it. But I think Sarah's presence restrained the young man somewhat. That's Sarah Hewett I'm talking about; she's my sister-in-law. She lives here. We took her and her daughter in after my brother died.''

Witherspoon glanced at Barnes to see if he was taking notes. The constable was scribbling furiously in his little brown book. Satisfied that Barnes would remind him to question Sarah Hewett, he turned and gave Mrs. Dapeers an encouraging smile. "Do go on, madam."

"Let's see; aside from the gentlemen from the brewery, Tom and Joanne were there when I came in." She frowned. "No, I tell another lie. They came in right after I did; I remember noticing Joanne's dress as she came into the pub. Though, again, I've no idea why Haydon invited them, he didn't much care for either Tom or his wife."

"But isn't Mr. Tom Dapeers your late husband's brother?" Barnes asked.

"Yes, but they didn't much like one another. They haven't been close for years." She smiled brightly. "In addition, they're rival pub owners. Like us, they own several pubs. I expect Haydon only invited them because he wanted to rub their noses in it a bit."

Perplexed, Witherspoon stared at her. "Rub their noses in it?" he repeated.

"In the fact that he was opening a pub less than a hundred yards away from one of their pubs," she clarified. "Haydon was like that, you see, never content just to do something, he always wanted to outdo his competition. Especially when the competition was his own brother."

"Anyone else, madam?" he asked, shocked to his very core. He wasn't so much surprised at the late Haydon Dapeers's rather dismal character. Witherspoon had observed that people who got themselves murdered frequently had rather awful character flaws. But he was stunned at the widow's casual cheerfulness in recounting her husband's pettiness. Moira Dapeers wasn't just being honest with them, she was positively enjoying herself.

"Well, all the local merchants and shopkeepers were there," she continued. "And the architect who redesigned the inside of the pub. But he didn't stay long. He had no reason to, Haydon had already paid him. I think that's about it—no, wait, I'm forgetting that awful little man at the bar." She pursed her lips in disgust. "There was the most disreputable-looking fellow there when we arrived. Quite dirty, actually. He and Haydon were talking. It surprised me, really. I was sure Haydon was going to toss him out, but he didn't."

"Do you know this man's name?" Witherspoon asked hopefully. None of the statements he'd looked at this morning at the Yard had mentioned a "dirty person."

"I've no idea who he was. But he was gone before Haydon was killed, I know that. I saw him leave. Rather portly little man, he had red hair and was wearing the filthiest porkpie hat I've ever seen."

"Would you recognize him again if you saw him?" Barnes asked. He glanced at the inspector.

"I expect so," she replied eagerly. "I did get rather a good look at him."

Constable Barnes cleared his throat. "Mrs. Dapeers, you said your husband owned three pubs. Was Mr. Dapeers well liked by his employees?"

"Goodness no." She giggled coquettishly and batted her eyelashes at the astounded-looking constable. "He was an impossible man. Look at the way he treated poor Mr. Taggert! Got the fellow to spend hours on those windows and then wouldn't pay him."

"He refused to pay wages?" Barnes queried.

"He paid eventually," Mrs. Dapeers said. "But never a minute before he had to and he was a real Tartar to work for. Haydon sacked people all the time."

Witherspoon's head was spinning. He'd never met a widow quite like Mrs. Dapeers. He wasn't sure if he was up to any more questions right at the moment. "Mrs. Dapeers," he said politely, "may we have a word with your sister-in-law?"

*   *   *

Dr. Bosworth's dark brown eyes regarded Mrs. Jeffries steadily as they sat across from one another at Lyons Tea Shop in Oxford Circus. "Actually, it was a fairly simple killing," he said. "There's nothing in the least mysterious about the death itself. The poor chap was stabbed from the back. The knife went straight into the heart. He died almost instantly."

Mrs. Jeffries nodded. She'd sent Dr. Bosworth a note early this morning asking him to meet her here. "There was no sign of a struggle or anything like that?"

"No," Bosworth replied slowly. "Not really. He had been hit on the head before he was stabbed, but the post-mortem revealed that the blow didn't do any real damage. It only stunned him for a moment or two. I don't think he knew what was happening until it was too late. Whoever killed him crept up from behind, banged him on the head and shoved the knife straight in. The blade pierced the heart; death would have been very swift."

"Were you able to determine what the killer used to hit him with?"

"No," Bosworth admitted honestly. "The wound only barely broke the skin; there wasn't any particular shape to it and no indentation at all on the skull. But I saw nothing lying about the room where the body was found that had blood on it. I know, because I had a good look round when the inspector and the constable stepped out of the room."

"I see." She fingered the white linen serviette in her lap. So far, she hadn't learned anything from the good doctor that she hadn't already heard from the inspector. Drat. "Was there anything special about the knife?" she asked.

"Not that I could see." Bosworth picked up his tea and took a huge gulp. "It appeared to be a standard kitchen knife; the blade was a good ten inches long. It was very sharp.''

"I wonder if the murderer brought it with him?'' Mrs. Jeffries mused. She made a mental note to try to find out. If the knife was already on the premises, then it could mean that the killer simply acted on the spur of the moment. But if the knife wasn't already in the pub, that meant the killer brought it with him, presumably with the intention of using it.

"Difficult to say.'' Bosworth yawned. "Oh sorry, but I've been up most of the night doing the postmortem on this one. Actually, as I said, it appears to be a very simple killing. But I will say that whoever murdered Dapeers was very lucky.''

"Lucky? How?''

"With his aim. The knife could just as easily have gone into the victim's back and not hit the heart, in which case, the man might not have died so quickly.''

She wondered if that was important. "But surely, stabbing someone in the back guarantees certain death.''

"Not necessarily,'' Bosworth said enthusiastically. "When I was in America, I once treated a miner who'd been in a brawl on the Barbary Coast. Fellow had walked about half the night with a knife sticking out of him, didn't bother to come see me till the next morning. He actually survived. The human body is a lot stronger than most people realize.''

Mrs. Jeffries knew he wasn't exaggerating. Dr. Bosworth had worked and studied in the United States; specifically, in San Francisco. The knowledge he'd garnered in that turbulent city gave him a depth of experience with violent death that was unsurpassed by any police surgeon in London. As Bosworth had once told her, "There's no shortage of murder and corpses in America.''

"Are you saying that the killer might have known precisely where to stab the victim?" she asked eagerly. Finally, she was getting to something important.

He shrugged. "It's certainly possible. There's quite a number of stabbings here in our own fair city that don't result in death. It could well be that the killer knows something about human anatomy. That knife entered the victim's back directly behind the heart. It could have been sheer luck on the killer's part, or he or she could have known exactly what they were doing."

"Gracious, if that were true," she replied, "then the killer would probably be someone who has studied medicine."

Bosworth laughed. "I wouldn't go that far—your killer could just as easily be a butcher or was just plain lucky. But it's something to think about. The knife virtually pierced the heart at the very center. Good aim, I'd say."

Disappointed, Mrs. Jeffries sighed. For once, they had Dr. Bosworth actually doing the postmortem instead of that idiot Dr. Potter, and the cause of death was so clear-cut and simple that it didn't make any difference. For all the good it did them, they might as well have had old Potter bumbling about with the body. "Is there anything else you think might be important?"

Bosworth hesitated and a slow flush crept up his pale cheeks. "Well," he said slowly, "there is something else, but it's most indelicate of me to mention it to a lady."

As his face was now as red as his hair, Mrs. Jeffries knew she was onto something. Eagerly, she leaned forward. "Now don't be silly, Doctor. There isn't much in this world that shocks me. Please, tell me."

He looked about him to ensure the patrons at the nearby tables weren't likely to overhear. "I don't know if this has anything to do with Dapeers's murder, but I did find something else when I was examining the body.''

''What was it?''

Bosworth dropped his gaze and stared at his half-full teacup. ''When I got inside the fellow, there were certain peculiarities—deterioration of tissue and that sort of thing.''

''You mean he was diseased.''

''Not just diseased.'' Bosworth finally looked up. ''He was dying.''

''Dying? Of what?''

Bosworth blushed again. ''It's not very nice.''

''No disease that I've ever heard of is 'nice,' '' she said, trying hard to keep her impatience in check. ''What was it? More importantly, do you think Dapeers knew he was dying?''

''He knew he had it all right,'' Bosworth said bluntly. ''The disease was advanced enough that he must have known it.''

''For goodness' sakes, what was his illness? Tuberculosis?'' A pub owner wouldn't want people to know if he had TB, she thought.

''No, that isn't it.'' Bosworth took another quick glance around the room and then leaned toward Mrs. Jeffries. ''Haydon Dapeers had syphilis.''

''I'm Sarah Hewett,'' the lovely young woman announced as she came into the drawing room. ''Moira said you wanted to speak to me.''

Sarah Hewett hadn't bothered to wear black. Her dress was pale lavender broadcloth, rather worn from one washing too many.

''Yes, I did.'' The inspector introduced Constable Barnes. ''I'm so sorry to intrude, but we must ask you some questions.''

"I understand." Sarah sat down in the chair her sister-in-law had just vacated. "I don't think I can be of much help, though. I didn't see anything."

Witherspoon smiled kindly at her. "How long have you lived here?" He thought getting a bit of background information might be helpful.

"Just a few months," Sarah replied. She clamped her hands together in her lap. "I was married to Moira's brother, Charles. He died last year. Haydon and Moira insisted my daughter and I come and live with them."

"How old is your daughter?" Witherspoon didn't think that had anything to do with the murder, but getting this young woman to relax might help her to talk more freely.

Sarah smiled widely. "She's two and a half."

"I understand you were at the Gilded Lily Pub last night when the murder occurred."

She nodded. "As were a number of other people. But as I told you, I didn't see anything. We were all watching the brawl on the street when Haydon went into the taproom. No one even noticed he was missing until Joanne tried to find him to say good night."

"I see." Witherspoon thought hard about what to ask next. "Er, were you standing with Mrs. Dapeers while you were watching the altercation?"

She hesitated briefly. "Well, no. Actually, as soon as I saw all that blood, I went back to the bar to get another glass of ale. It was quite warm, you see. I was thirsty."

"And did the barman serve you?"

"No, he'd come out from behind the bar and gone to stand at the front door." She smiled slightly. "I guess he was curious as to what was going on outside too."

"Did you see anyone going down the hall or into the taproom while you were at the bar?" Witherspoon asked.

"I wasn't paying any attention." She shrugged. "Be-

sides, I didn't go to the bar right away. I went to the front
door with everyone else when we heard the shouting start,
but I got pushed outside in the crush. As soon as I saw that
drayman smash the cabbie's nose and all that blood started
running down his face, I couldn't stand it, so I went back
inside. But I had to push my way in; it took quite a few
minutes.''

"Did anyone else come inside with you?" he pressed.

"A couple of other people drifted in, but I don't remember who they were. As I told you, I wasn't paying any
attention. It was hot and I was tired. Frankly, Inspector, I
wanted nothing more than to find something to drink and
go home. I wasn't there to have a good time, I was there
because Haydon insisted I come.''

"Did you talk to anyone during this time?"

"During what time?" she asked irritably.

"While you were at the bar," he explained patiently.
"Did you speak to anyone?"

"No."

"What about Mr. Taggert?"

"He was still outside," she said quickly. "I remember
that.''

"What makes you so certain?" Witherspoon asked curiously.

She said nothing for a moment and the inspector had the
distinct impression she was trying to think of what to say.
Finally, she said, "I remember because I had to brush past
him as I came back inside. He stepped aside to let me
pass.''

"I see. Mrs. Hewett, were you present when Mr. Taggert
had words with your brother-in-law?"

"I don't know what you mean, Inspector. What kind of
'words'?"

"Specifically, did you hear Mr. Taggert threaten Mr. Dapeers because Mr. Dapeers hadn't paid him for his work?''

"He didn't threaten Haydon," she cried. "At least not with murder.''

"So you were present," Witherspoon pressed.

Sarah Hewett looked down at her lap. "All right, I'll admit I was there. But all Michael said was that if Haydon didn't pay him, he'd have him in court. He didn't threaten him with violence.''

"Did Mr. Dapeers threaten Mr. Taggert with violence?'' Barnes interjected.

"No, he just asked Michael to leave. But Moira came over just then and she likes Michael. Haydon couldn't keep making a fuss in front of her, so Michael stayed.''

"And were the two of you together until the fight broke out on the street?'' the inspector asked. He found it significant that she referred to him as "Michael" and not "Mr. Taggert.''

"Yes," Sarah replied firmly. "That's why I know he couldn't have had anything to do with Haydon's murder. He was with me the whole time until I came back into the pub. And he didn't come in after me, either. I would have noticed him.''

Witherspoon studied Sarah Hewett carefully. Her chin was lifted defiantly, her gaze steady and direct. Though he wasn't terribly experienced at matters of the heart, recent events in his own personal life had made him more sensitive to certain situations. This young woman was bound and determined not to say a word to incriminate Michael Taggert. He decided to try a different tactic. "Did your brother-in-law have enemies?''

Surprised by the question, she drew back slightly. "Enemies?'' she repeated.

"Yes, people who didn't much like him,'' the inspector explained.

"I know what the word means, Inspector," Sarah replied. "I was merely surprised at your bluntness. But yes, Haydon did have enemies."

"Who? Can you give us any names?"

"That would take too long, Inspector." She smiled slightly. "But I think I can safely say that just about everyone who knew Haydon disliked him intensely. Apparently, someone disliked him enough to kill him."

CHAPTER 3

————∞◦∞————

"You can get a decent pint at one of Haydon Dapeers's pubs," said Dick, a street lad who couldn't have been more than sixteen. He nodded knowingly. "Not like the swill they serve at the Black Horse. Stuff's not fit to drink, tastes like cat's piss."

Wiggins nodded in agreement, as though he knew what the boy was talking about, which he didn't. He didn't think Dick knew all that much about it, either. But at least he'd found someone to talk to, someone who'd been hanging about the streets when the murder took place and seemed to know the victim. "So Haydon Dapeers was a nice gent, then?"

"Nice?" The lad snorted in disbelief. "I never said that! He was a right mean ol' bastard. Most folks round these parts couldn't stand him. But he does serve decent ale. I heard his new place is right posh, not like here. Peeked in through the windows last evenin', but I didn't go in or anythin'."

They were sitting in the public bar of the Pale Swan, another pub owned by the late Haydon Dapeers. It was an ordinary public house with white-painted walls, hardwood floors and high beamed ceilings. Wiggins rather liked it.

"How come people didn't like 'im?" Wiggins asked. He dug in his pocket, pulled out a few coins and nodded to the barman, signaling they'd like another round. Cor, he didn't think Mrs. Jeffries would much like him drinkin' all this beer, not while he was askin' questions. But it was bloomin' 'ot outside and the only way he could get anyone to tell 'im anything was by buyin' 'em a drink.

The barman brought them two more light ales. "Drink up, lads," he said genially, scooping up the coins and moving on down the half-empty bar.

"This is right nice of ya," Dick said, grabbing his glass and taking a huge gulp.

"Got nothin' else to do today. Might as well 'ave a beer or two, seein' as it's so 'ot outside," Wiggins replied. "Now, you were tellin' me about Haydon Dapeers not bein' so popular round 'ere."

"It's no surprise 'e got murdered." Dick glanced quickly around the room. "He 'ad plenty of enemies, that's for sure."

"Who?"

"His own brother, for starters," Dick replied with relish. "I know that for a fact, 'cause Tom Dapeers give me a job moving the empty barrels in the taproom. This was yesterday morning, it was. While I was in there Haydon Dapeers showed up at their pub and they had the most awful dustup."

"They 'ad a fight?"

"Nah." Dick laughed. "Dapeers weren't the type to use his fists. It were an argument. But I 'eard Mr. Tom screamin' at Dapeers that it was all a ruddy lie, and if he tried spreadin' it around, he'd see Dapeers in court.''

Wiggins nodded thoughtfully. ''What was they on about?''

Dick shrugged. ''Don't know. I only heard part of the row. Then Mrs. Tom come in and Haydon left. But I don't reckon it means anything. Mr. Tom and Mr. Haydon didn't act much like brothers, if you know what I mean. They couldn't really stick each other. Mrs. Joanne, she really 'ated Mr. Haydon. Especially when she found out he was goin' to be openin' that fancy pub right up the road from their place. She went on and on about it. Claimed Mr. Haydon were doin' it on purpose just to ruin their trade. Mind you''—Dick took another quick drink and wiped his mouth with the back of his hand—''if you ask me, she was dead right. Mr. Haydon probably was tryin' to ruin their business.''

''Guess the brother and his missus didn't get invited to the opening of the Gilded Lily.'' Wiggins laughed.

''That's the strange part,'' Dick said eagerly. ''They did. I saw 'em walkin' right into the Gilded Lily yesterday evenin'. Mrs. Joanne was all dressed up like she was goin' to the opera or somethin', and Mr. Tom was wearin' a suit and tie.''

''It's a wonder Haydon Dapeers didn't toss 'em out.''

''That's what I thought,'' Dick said eagerly. ''I was sure I'd see them come right back out again. 'Corse I was curious, so I had a gander through the window, you know, lookin' to see if Dapeers would boot 'em out. Well, I saw him talkin' to them all nice like, as though the argument at the Black Horse had never happened.''

''That's right strange,'' Wiggins said thoughtfully. ''Guess they musta made it up.''

Dick shrugged again. ''Reckon so. Either that, or Mr. Tom and his wife was so eager to see the inside of the place, they were willin' to swallow their pride.''

Wiggins belched softly. ''Sounds like an awful lot of trouble to go to just to get a look at the place,'' he mused. ''Why didn't they just look in the windows while the pub was bein' fitted out?''

Dick laughed. ''Oh, you wouldna seen nothin'. Mr. Haydon kept the windows covered in brown paper the whole time the work was bein' done on it.''

Wiggins took another swallow of beer, grimacing as the brew slipped down his throat. He felt awfully dizzy. He glanced down at his feet and thought the floor looked a long ways away. When he looked up again, Dick's twin brother seemed to be sitting right next to Dick. Even worse, the room was starting to spin.

Betsy studied the young man behind the counter of the grocer shop on Tottenham Road. He wasn't very attractive. He looked the sort of man who would be flattered by a little attention. Short and rather portly with a head of frizzy dark hair and skin so pale it reminded her of a fish's belly, he wore thick, wire-rimmed spectacles that couldn't quite hide his bushy eyebrows and a rumpled white shirt beneath his grocer's apron. She ignored the jab at her conscience because she was being so cold-bloodedly deliberate in picking her choice of prey. But there was a murder to solve. ''Excuse me, sir.'' She smiled warmly. ''But I was wondering if I might trouble you a moment?''

He blinked at her from behind his spectacles, as though he was surprised she was speaking to him. ''Uh, of course, miss. What can I do for you?''

''Do you know where the Dapeers residence might be?''

''We're not allowed to give out that sort of thing about our customers,'' he said, blushing all the way to the roots of his hair.

"Oh," she sighed dramatically. "That's too bad. My mistress wanted me to take a letter of condolence around to Mrs. Dapeers, but I've lost the address."

"Terrible business, that," the clerk said.

"Yes." She shuddered delicately. "Dreadful, isn't it? Imagine being stabbed in your own pub."

"And on the opening day too!" he agreed, glancing at the back of the shop to see if his employer was lurking about.

She leaned closer across the counter. "It makes a body scared to walk the streets, it does." She sighed again and made her shoulders droop slightly. "And here I've got to try and find that poor woman's address. . . ."

"It's all right, now," the clerk said quickly. "I think I can help you out. The Dapeers house is at number twenty-eight Percy Road. It's just round the corner."

"Thank you, ever so much. You've saved me an awful lot of bother."

He blushed even redder. "Mrs. Dapeers and her sister-in-law come in here every now and again. They're both nice ladies."

"It must be terrible for her, losing her husband like that."

"Yes," he agreed solemnly. "But just between you and me and a tin of sugar, I doubt that there's many who'll shed any tears at his funeral."

Betsy gazed at him appreciatively. "You mean he wasn't well liked?"

"Not by anyone who worked for him. My sister worked for the Dapeers household a few months ago and she finally left."

"Goodness, why? Didn't he pay proper wages?"

"Hamilton," a booming voice from the rear of the shop bellowed. "Are you through serving that young lady?"

"Almost, sir." Hamilton smiled nervously at Betsy. "Will there be anything else, miss?"

Betsy didn't want to get him into trouble. She might not be above a bit of flirting to find out what she needed to know, but she wasn't going to cause someone to lose their position. "Just that tin of cocoa, there," she said.

He smiled gratefully at her as he turned and pulled a tin of Cadbury's off the shelf. "Anything else, miss?" he said loudly enough for his employer to hear.

"No, thank you." Betsy gave him another smile. "And I appreciate all your help," she said, stressing the last word ever so slightly.

Hamilton busied himself with taking her money and casting furtive glances toward the rear of the shop to see if he was still being watched. But the owner of the shop, a tall, thin man with graying hair and a long, taciturn face, kept his eye on the clerk and Betsy.

Blast, she thought as she saw the proprietor start toward the front of the shop, what bad luck. Just when she'd finally made contact with someone who might know something about Dapeers, this old Tartar has to ruin everything! She decided to try one last thing.

"Excuse me," she said softly. Hamilton looked up from wrapping her tin of cocoa in brown paper. Betsy gave him a bold smile. "But I don't suppose you know of any nice pubs round here, do you?" she asked innocently.

Tom Dapeers smiled uncertainly at the two policemen. He didn't much like policemen hanging about his pub, but as these two were investigating old Haydon's murder, he could hardly ask them to leave. "I don't know what we can tell you," he said. "Joanne and I only went round to the place for a few minutes. We didn't see anything."

Inspector Witherspoon sighed silently. No one seemed to

have seen anything. He glanced at Constable Barnes, who was staring longingly at a glass of pale ale sitting on the far end of the bar. "Exactly what time did you arrive?"

"It must have been a few minutes before six," Tom replied.

"It were a quarter to," Mrs. Dapeers put in. "I remember because I looked at the time right before we left here."

"And did you speak to Mr. Dapeers once you got to the Gilded Lily?" Witherspoon asked.

"Of course," Tom said. "We were guests. You can't go to a man's place of business and not talk to him."

"Did Mr. Dapeers seem to be in his usual frame of mind?"

Mrs. Dapeers's eyebrows drew together. "What do you mean by that?"

"I mean, did he appear to be upset about anything?" Witherspoon thought it a perfectly reasonable question.

"He was happier than a pig in swill," Mrs. Dapeers shot back. "Nothing Haydon liked more than showing off. And that new pub of his was his pride and joy." She laughed harshly. "He'd invited the whole neighborhood to come see it. Mind you, I don't care how fancy the place is, it don't hold a candle to ours."

Witherspoon thought that remark strange. The Black Horse Pub, while clean and decent enough, was as plain as a pikestaff compared with the Gilded Lily. But he certainly wouldn't be rude enough to contradict a lady. "While you were there, did you see or hear Mr. Dapeers do anything unusual?"

Tom frowned slightly. "Well, not that I can remember."

"Haydon was talking to that dirty little man in the porkpie hat," Joanne interrupted. "Funny-looking fellow, don't your remember him, Tom? He was standing at the far end of the bar. When Haydon first went over to talk to him, I thought he was going to throw him out. But he didn't, he stood there and had quite a chat with the bloke.'' She grinned maliciously. ''And I don't think he liked what the man had to say, either. By the time the fellow left, Haydon's mouth was open so far, I thought he'd trip over his chin.''

''You think that this man said something that upset Mr. Dapeers?'' Witherspoon pressed.

''I know he did.''

''Now, Joanne,'' her husband protested, ''you're just guessing. It could be that Haydon was still upset by that set-to he had with young Taggert.''

Witherspoon made a mental note to remind himself to ask a few more questions about the dirty man in the porkpie hat. But that could come later. ''Did you see this, er, set-to between Mr. Taggert and the victim?'' he asked.

''Only a little of it,'' Tom began. ''Mr. Jenkins, the owner of the butcher shop down the street, waved me over to the bar about the time they was really getting heated with one another, so I only heard the beginning of the row.''

''I saw and heard the whole thing, Inspector,'' his wife said firmly. ''Mind you, Haydon and Taggert weren't troublin' to keep their voices down; you could hear them quite clearly, even over all the noise in the pub.''

''Taggert's an artist,'' Tom added. ''Haydon hired him to etch all that fancy stuff on the windows in the pub. Nice young fellow, I don't know why he took that job with Haydon in the first place. He studied in Italy, you know. Comes from a good family too. There's money there somewhere, you can always tell, you know.''

Barnes cast a quick look at the inspector. ''What was the argument about?''

''Haydon hadn't paid the man,'' Tom explained. ''At

least the bit I heard was about money. Mind you, I'm not surprised. Haydon had a bit of reputation for not paying people when he owed them.''

Joanne snorted. ''Don't be daft,'' she told her husband. ''It was more than that. I was standing right behind them and I heard everything. Michael Taggert wasn't just lookin' for his money, he was warning Haydon to leave Sarah alone.''

''Joanne!'' Tom glared at his wife. ''It's not decent to say such things.''

''It's the truth.'' She shrugged, totally unconcerned by her husband's disapproval. ''The old goat never could keep his hands to himself.''

Witherspoon sincerely hoped he wasn't blushing. Gracious, this case was getting complicated. ''Are you saying that Haydon Dapeers was trying to force his attentions on his own sister-in-law?''

Joanne Dapeers stared him directly in the eye, not in the least embarrassed to be speaking bluntly about such a delicate matter. ''That's exactly what I'm saying. He was a disgusting man, Haydon was, always after the young women. Only this time Michael wasn't having it.''

''I take it Mr. Taggert, er . . .''

''He's in love with Sarah Hewett,'' Joanne finished. ''And I expect now that Haydon's dead, he'll ask her to marry him.''

''Mrs. Hewett is a widow, isn't she?'' Barnes asked. ''So why does Mr. Dapeers's death have any bearing on whether or not she remarries?''

Joanne shrugged. ''I don't know. Sarah hated having to live with Haydon and Moira, not that she had anything against Moira. She's a nice enough woman. A bit wrapped up in her charity work and the missionary society, but she was always kind to Sarah. It was Haydon Sarah couldn't stomach. I know for a fact that Michael Taggert's been after Sarah to marry him and I know that Sarah loves Michael too. But for some strange reason, she kept putting him off.''

Tom frowned at his wife. ''You shouldn't be repeating gossip, Joanne.''

''Why not if it's true?'' she queried.

Confused, Witherspoon asked, ''Excuse me, Mrs. Dapeers. But are you merely repeating what others have told you about Mr. Taggert and Mrs. Hewett's relationship? Or do you have knowledge of your own about the matter?''

''Am I under oath, then?'' she asked irritably. ''Despite what my husband says, I'm not repeating gossip. I know bloody good and well that Michael Taggert wanted to marry Sarah, because he told me so himself. He also told me that she loved him but she kept putting him off and wouldn't tell him why. He was sure it was because of some nastiness that Haydon was up to. Now, if you don't believe me, you can ask him yourself.''

''When did Mr. Taggert tell you all this?'' Witherspoon asked.

''Last week,'' she replied. ''He used to come in here after he'd finished working at the Gilded Lily. He's a nice young man and we chatted quite a bit. He told me all about him and Sarah.''

''What time is the inspector due home?'' Betsy asked as she laid the table for late-afternoon tea.

''I'm not sure,'' Mrs. Jeffries replied. ''You know he keeps such irregular hours when he's on a murder.''

''I hope he's not expectin' a big cooked dinner,'' Mrs. Goodge grumbled. She put a plate of sliced brown bread on the table next to the teapot. ''It's too hot to do much cookin' and I've been busy today. I've had to send word to all my sources and I'm not sure it'll do much good.''

"Of course it will," Mrs. Jeffries soothed. The cook was obviously still annoyed that their latest victim was only a mere publican. Mrs. Jeffries didn't much blame her. Not that she felt a publican was any less important than a member of the aristocracy, it was just that it was so much easier to find out gossip about the upper classes. They were so much more visible and they had far larger households than the lower classes. For once, she felt very sympathetic to Mrs. Goodge's plight. It was a bit like her own. Mrs. Jeffries hadn't exactly found out much today either. She certainly hoped the rest of them would have something worthwhile to report.

"Has anyone heard from Luty or Hatchet?" Betsy asked. She pulled her chair out and sat down, grateful to be off her feet. Her head was sore from the beer she'd had at the pub and her stomach was upset. But she was delighted with what she'd found out. If she was very clever, she could find out ever so much information when she met with Hamilton tomorrow. His sister had worked for the Dapeerses, she was bound to know something.

"Smythe sent them a telegram early this morning," Mrs. Jeffries replied. "I shouldn't be surprised if they show up tomorrow."

"But they'll have only arrived!" Mrs. Goodge exclaimed. "Surely they'll not turn round and come straight back."

"Would you like to bet on that?" Betsy asked. "I don't think either of them really wanted to go in the first place."

There was a loud noise as the back door slammed shut. Fred, hearing the sound of familiar footsteps, leapt up and took off in a dead run toward the back hall.

"Down, boy," Wiggins cried. "You'll knock me over if you're not careful."

"Wiggins is back," Betsy muttered. She turned and saw

the footman stumbling toward the table. The dog was bouncing around his feet and it was all he could do to keep from tripping. "Are you all right?" she asked. The lad was pale as a sheet; he was breathing heavily and he was clutching his stomach.

"What's wrong with you, boy?" Mrs. Goodge asked crossly.

"Oh . . ." He moaned and launched himself toward the kitchen table. "I've got to sit down, I don't feel well."

"Gracious, Wiggins, are you ill?" Mrs. Jeffries asked in alarm.

He landed heavily in his seat. "I'm just a bit off-color," he belched softly. The smell of beer wafted off him.

"Have you been drinking?" Betsy demanded.

He hiccuped. "Well, only a little . . ." He clutched his stomach again and tried to rise to his feet. "If you don't mind, Mrs. Jeffries, I don't think I want any tea."

"You're drunk," Mrs. Goodge snapped.

"And feeling the worse for it," Mrs. Jeffries said kindly.

Wiggins moaned. "It's not my fault. The only way to get people in pubs to talk is to pour beer down their throat."

"I think you'd better go have a lay-down," Mrs. Jeffries said.

"That's a good idea." He belched again, got to his feet and stumbled out of the kitchen.

"Well, I never," Mrs. Goodge exclaimed. "What would the inspector say!"

"I don't really think that's the sort of thing we ought to tell him," Mrs. Jeffries said blandly. "Let the lad sleep it off. We'll talk to him at dinner tonight and see what he's learned."

"So it's just the three of us," Betsy said cheerfully. She too had been in a pub, but unlike Wiggins, she'd been very careful about how much ale she'd poured down her throat. She didn't really like the taste of alcohol all that much. Besides, she was scared of liquor. She'd seen too many gin-soaked women when she was growing up in the East End.

"Perhaps Smythe will be along soon," Mrs. Jeffries said. "I've no idea what he's off doing."

"I've been doin' the same as you lot," Smythe's voice came from the kitchen door. "Investigatin' this murder."

Betsy turned her head sharply. "We didn't hear you come in."

"I came in the front door," he admitted, grinning at the maid and sauntering over to take his seat.

Mrs. Goodge gave him a quick, disapproving glance. Household servants were not supposed to use the front door! But she held her tongue.

Mrs. Jeffries and Mrs. Goodge took their places at the table. "I'm glad you're back, we've quite a bit to talk about."

"Where's Wiggins?" Smythe asked. "Isn't 'e back yet?"

Betsy giggled. "He's upstairs having a sleep. He's been drinking! Claims that's the only way to get people to talk to him."

"Load of rubbish, that is," the cook grumbled. "You don't see me pouring alcohol down people's throats to get them to loosen their tongues."

"You've found something out, then?" Smythe asked innocently. He was fairly certain that Mrs. Goodge hadn't found out a ruddy thing. Otherwise she wouldn't be so bloomin' irritated.

"Have some tea, Smythe," Mrs. Jeffries said briskly. She didn't want them to start bickering with one another. "And I'll tell everyone what I learned from Dr. Bosworth."

She poured the tea, passed the plate of bread and butter and told them about her meeting with Bosworth. "So you see, there really isn't all that much to tell," she concluded a few minutes later. "But according to the doctor, either the killer was lucky or he might have known something about human anatomy."

"I reckon the killer was lucky," Smythe said. "From what I found out today, there weren't no one in that pub that knew a bloomin' thing about anatomy."

"You found out who all was there?" Betsy asked.

Smythe shook his head. "That's what I've spent most of today doin'." He fumbled in his pocket and drew out a crumpled sheet of paper. "Got their names written right here."

"Goodness, Smythe, that was resourceful of you," Mrs. Jeffries said eagerly. "Now we've at least got a complete list of suspects."

Smythe didn't bother to tell them that the list had cost him a pretty penny. "Not quite a complete list, Mrs. Jeffries. I had a word with Mick, the barman who was workin' last night. There were a number of people left in the public bar when Dapeers was killed." He frowned, trying to make out his own writing. "Mick didn't know all their names, but I reckon the killer must 'ave been someone who was known to Dapeers, so I'm 'opin' that the names that's missin' aren't important."

"Hmm," Mrs. Jeffries said doubtfully. "I suppose a partial list is better than none. Who is on it?"

Smythe squinted at the crinkled paper. "There was Mick and Molly, of course, they worked for Dapeers. Tom and Joanne Dapeers, that's Haydon Dapeers's younger brother and his wife. Sarah Hewett, that's Dapeers's sister-in-law, and Moira Dapeers, the victim's wife. Two fellows from Bestal's Brewery, Luther Pump and Edward Magil. John

Rowland, he owns the little hotel next door to the pub, he was there. Michael Taggert, he's the artist that did all the fancy etching on the pub windows, and Horace Bell, he owns the livery down the road from the Gilded Lily.'' Smythe paused for a breath and then continued reading the names.

"There was over twenty people in that pub when the murder took place," Betsy exclaimed when he'd finished. "And no one saw a ruddy thing!"

"But that's just it," Smythe said patiently. "They weren't *in* the pub. They was outside watching a brawl between a cabbie and a drayman. Musta been a good fight too; the copper from the corner had to come down and break it up."

"I wonder if the people in the Gilded Lily were all personal friends of Dapeers," Mrs. Jeffries mused. "Or were they just customers?"

"Both," Smythe answered. "Mick told me that Dapeers had asked most of them to come around seein' as 'ow it was 'is birthday, but a few of the people 'ad come in just to 'ave a look at the place too. Mick told me Dapeers was a bit worried when the crowd started comin' in; there was some trouble with the beer. Seems there wasn't enough on hand, the brewery hadn't delivered enough."

"I'll bet that's why the men from Bestal's were there," Betsy said.

"That certainly sounds logical," Mrs. Jeffries agreed. "Did you learn anything else, Smythe?"

"Not really." The coachman picked up his mug of tea. " 'Ow did the rest of you do?"

"I'm meeting a woman who used to work for Dapeers tomorrow," Betsy said proudly. "Hamilton promised he'd bring his sister along to the Six Gates after he got off work. But I didn't find out all that much today. Hamilton couldn't really remember much of what his sister had told him about Dapeers. All he knew was that Dapeers was always onto his wife about her giving her money away to some missionary society.''

"You've done better than I have," Mrs. Goodge said morosely. "I didn't learn anything. No one's heard of Haydon Dapeers. I've sent word to every source I've got and there's nothing. Absolutely nothing.''

Michael Taggert lived in the ground-floor flat of a small, redbrick house in Chelsea. "I thought you'd be around soon," he said as he opened the door wider and motioned for Inspector Witherspoon and Constable Barnes to step inside.

The room was messy: clothes were strewn on the furniture, a half-finished painting stood on an easel next to the window and the linen on the daybed in the corner was tangled in a heap. "You'll have to forgive the mess, gentlemen," Taggert said, "but I've been working and I haven't had time to tidy up.''

"You're an artist, Mr. Taggert?" Witherspoon asked politely.

"Yes," Taggert replied. He shoved a heap of newspapers off the settee. "At least I'm trying to be. Please sit down," he invited. The two policemen sat down.

"I expect you know why we're here," Witherspoon began. Taggert nodded. "So I'll get right to it. You were at the Gilded Lily Pub yesterday evening, is that correct?"

"Yes.''

"Were you an invited guest?" Barnes asked.

Taggert grinned. "I'm the last person that Haydon Dapeers would have invited. But I was there anyway.''

"Would you tell us why?" Witherspoon asked.

"Two reasons." Taggert held up two fingers. "One, I

wanted to see Sarah Hewett, and two, I wanted to collect the money that Haydon owed me.''

"Dapeers owed you money?" Witherspoon said. Of course, he already knew this, but he'd found that sometimes pretending that one didn't know something was the very best way of getting an enormous amount of information out of a suspect. And frankly, from what the inspector had heard today, Michael Taggert was the only suspect he had.

"I'd done quite a bit of work for Dapeers," Taggert explained. "He hired me to etch the designs on the glass partitions in the pub and to do the carving on the wood panels behind the bar.''

"I thought you were a painter, sir," Barnes said, glancing at the canvas near the window. He couldn't see what was on the thing, only the back of the easel.

"Painting is my main interest," Taggert said, "but I do a few other things as well. I'd done this work for Dapeers, finished it last week, but Dapeers wouldn't pay me.''

"Why?"

"How should I know why?" Taggert exclaimed. "He was a tightfisted sod, but I didn't think he'd stoop so low as to not pay what he owed.''

"Did you threaten Mr. Dapeers?" Witherspoon asked quietly. Goodness, the man was certainly being honest. He didn't try to hide his true feelings about the victim.

Taggert hesitated. He crossed his arms over his chest and sighed. "Threaten? Yes, you could say that. I told him if he didn't pay what he owed, I'd have him in court.''

"Is that when Mr. Dapeers asked you to leave?" Witherspoon asked.

Taggert laughed harshly. "He tried to throw me out when I warned him to keep his hands off Sarah. But just then Mrs. Dapeers came along, so Haydon had to behave himself and pretend that we were just talking.''

Surprised by the man's honesty, Witherspoon stared at him. He'd rather expected Taggert to start lying about now. "He was forcing his attentions on this young woman?" he pressed.

"That's a polite way of saying he couldn't keep his bloody hands to himself." Taggert sneered. "Haydon hadn't actually gone so far as rape, but he wouldn't leave Sarah alone and she was trapped in that damned house with him. I was warning him off when Mrs. Dapeers came over."

"Did you threaten him?"

"I didn't have time," Taggert admitted. "Besides, Sarah didn't want me to make a scene. But Dapeers got my point."

"I take it you and Mrs. Hewett are, er, close friends," the inspector said.

Taggert's expression softened. "We're going to be married. I'm coming into an inheritance soon; the minute I get it I'm marrying Sarah and taking her and her daughter away from here."

Drat. The inspector sighed silently. There was something about Taggert that he rather liked. He was obviously very much in love with Sarah Hewett. Witherspoon glanced wistfully around the room, his lips creasing in a smile. He hoped the artist didn't turn out to be a murderer. Why, as a young man, the inspector had once entertained ideas about being an artist himself. Not that he'd been serious, of course. But still, he glanced longingly at the back of the easel, wondering what was on the canvas and whether or not Mr. Taggert would mind him having a quick peek. From behind him, he heard Constable Barnes clear his throat loudly. Witherspoon snapped his head around to Taggert. "Er, how long have you known Mrs. Hewett?" he asked. The question wasn't particularly pertinent to the case, but he might as well ask. One never knew what one could find out by a little digging.

"About three and a half years. Sarah was living with an aunt in Bayswater when we met. We would have married three years ago except that I had a chance to go to Italy to study and Sarah made me take it." He smashed his fist down on the table, rattling some dirty cups and making the two policemen jump. "I would to God I had married her then. Instead, she married Hewett and ended up widowed and having to live with that pig Dapeers. I'll never forgive myself for leaving her; never."

"Now, now, Mr. Taggert. Please calm yourself."

"Calm myself! Do you know what she's had to endure from that man?" he cried. "He never let her forget that she and her daughter were beholden to him. He taunted her with her poverty and watched her every move. She was a prisoner!"

"Why didn't you marry her when you came back from Italy?" Barnes asked softly.

"I couldn't," Taggert replied. "She refused me; she said I'd end up hating her and the child, because if we married, I'd have to give up my work and find employment. But that's not the case now. I've my inheritance."

Witherspoon found this all very fascinating, but it didn't have anything to do with Dapeers's murder. "Mr. Taggert, did you go outside to watch the brawl that broke out on the street?"

"The brawl was starting just as I was leaving," he replied, shaking his head. "I didn't stay around to watch it."

Witherspoon and Barnes exchanged glances.

"You and Mrs. Hewett didn't go outside together?" he persisted.

"No," Taggert said. "I was gone."

The inspector ignored that and pressed ahead with his

own questions. "Are you absolutely certain of when you left the pub?"

Puzzled, Taggert glanced from Barnes to Witherspoon. "Yes. Why? Did someone else tell you differently? The fight hadn't started yet; the cabbie was just starting to yell insults when I left."

"Where did you go?"

"I went for a walk." He folded his arms over his chest. "I was really angry, so angry I didn't trust myself to stay in the same room with Dapeers."

"Then how did you find out Dapeers had been murdered?" Witherspoon asked.

"From one of the barmaids at the Black Horse. I'd stopped in there for a drink."

"The Black Horse?" Witherspoon repeated. "Isn't that Tom Dapeers's pub?"

Taggert nodded slowly. "I drop by there every now and again. Tom's a nice man. Not at all like his brother. Hard to believe they come from the same stock."

"Which barmaid?" Barnes pressed.

"I don't know her name," Taggert replied. "She's just started working there. The other girl got sacked a couple of days ago."

"And that's when you found out that Dapeers had been murdered?" Witherspoon asked. He wasn't sure why he wanted to be absolutely clear on this point, but his "inner voice" was warning him it might be important. "When you dropped into the Black Horse?"

"Of course that's when I heard. Everyone was talking about it," Taggert said. "And none of them shedding any tears for him, either. Look, obviously you don't believe me. Did someone tell you I was at the Gilded Lily when the murder happened?"

Witherspoon hesitated briefly. "In a manner of speaking, yes. Someone did."

"Who?" Taggert asked belligerently. "I want to know who said I was there so I can call him a liar to his face."

"I'm afraid it wasn't a him, sir," Witherspoon said softly. "It was a her. It was Sarah Hewett."

"Would you care for more sherry, sir?" Mrs. Jeffries asked the inspector. Goodness, she thought, he wasn't very talkative this evening. "Dinner won't be ready for a few minutes, so you've plenty of time for another one."

"This one will do me fine, Mrs. Jeffries," the inspector replied, waving his half-full glass in her direction.

"How is the investigation going, sir?" she asked.

"Oh, we're moving right along."

"Did you manage to talk with the other suspects today?"

"Of course." He yawned. "Quite a busy day it was too. By the way, have you had any more letters from Lady Cannonberry?"

Drat, Mrs. Jeffries thought, he was changing the subject again. He'd done that twice since he'd come home. "Only a short note to tell us she was having a nice time. She enjoys the country, even if she isn't overly fond of her late husband's relatives."

Witherspoon frowned. "It's jolly decent of her to go at all. I was rather hoping she might have mentioned when she would be returning to London."

"She didn't say, sir. Did you find out—"

"Isn't it time for dinner yet?" Witherspoon queried. "I'm hungry enough to eat a horse."

Mrs. Jeffries gave up. She'd try again once the man had his stomach full.

CHAPTER 4

"I'm afraid the inspector wasn't very forthcoming last night," Mrs. Jeffries told the others at breakfast the next morning. "He didn't tell me very much." To be precise, he hadn't really told her anything worthwhile at all.

" 'Ow much is 'very much'?" Smythe asked cautiously.

"Well," Mrs. Jeffries said slowly, "I'm afraid he really didn't say anything at all."

"Nothing at all!" Mrs. Goodge exclaimed. "What's gotten into the man?"

Betsy reached for a slice of toast. "I'm not sure what you mean? Are you saying the inspector doesn't know anything or that he deliberately avoided answering your questions?"

"I mean," Mrs. Jeffries said irritably, "that he talked about everything under the sun except this murder case. I tried all my usual methods of questioning him, but he rather neatly sidestepped my queries. He kept asking me all sorts of silly questions about women's clothing."

"Maybe he was just tired," Wiggins suggested softly. He hadn't said more than three words to anyone since he'd come into the kitchen, bleary-eyed and clutching his stomach.

"He wasn't tired," Mrs. Jeffries replied flatly. "He was deliberately avoiding talking about the murder." She'd spent half the night worrying about the inspector's reticence and she'd finally come to the conclusion there was only one thing to do. Confront the man. Find out precisely why he'd closed up tighter than a bank vault.

"Maybe he's onto us," Smythe mused. "Maybe that last case . . ."

Mrs. Jeffries shook her head. "I don't think that's the problem. Last night he was muttering something about listening to his natural instincts, his inner voice—"

"What inner voice?" Mrs. Goodge interrupted. "Is he hearin' things now? My uncle Donald went like that when he was about the inspector's age. It happens sometimes. Out of the clear blue they start hearing things and then they start seeing things. That's when you've really got to keep a sharp eye on them; once they start seeing things that aren't there you've got to lock them up. Causes all sorts of problems."

"I'm hearin' things," Wiggins muttered, frowning as he turned to stare at the hall. "Either that, or Luty Belle and Hatchet's fixin' to come through the back door. I just 'eard a carriage pull up."

Fred, his tail wagging furiously, suddenly jumped up and dashed out of the kitchen. There was a loud pounding on the back door and, a moment later, footsteps in the hall.

"Good morning," Hatchet, Luty Belle Crookshank's dignified butler, called out. "Is anyone here?"

"Good Lord, Hatchet," Luty cried. "You should have waited till someone come to the door to let us in. We can't go bargin' in on folks at this time of the mornin'."

"We're not barging in, madam," Hatchet replied as he
came into the kitchen. "They sent us a telegram." He
stopped and smiled broadly, sure of his welcome. He was
a tall, distinguished, white-haired gentleman wearing an immaculate black suit and carrying a walking stick in one
hand while holding on to his old-fashioned top hat with the
other. "Hello, everyone, I do hope you don't mind us coming around this early. But I knew you'd be up and eager to
get cracking on our case."

"What he means," Luty said, shooting her butler a disgruntled glance, "is that he hoped you'd be up so he
wouldn't have to wait another minute to find out about this
murder we've got."

Luty Belle Crookshank was a white-haired, rich Ameri-
can. She was small of stature, sharp as a razor and had a
penchant for wearing outrageously bright clothes. Today
she had donned a brilliant blue day dress with a matching
hat, carried a parasol festooned with lacy rosettes and, of
course, her white fur muff. Luty never went anywhere without her muff. She carried a Colt .45 in it, despite both
Hatchet's and the household of Upper Edmonton Gardens'
pleas that it was dangerous. As Luty was fond of telling
them, her "Peacemaker" had gotten the inspector out of
trouble more than once in the past.

"Goodness," Mrs. Jeffries exclaimed, "how on earth did
you get here so fast?"

"Don't ask." Luty rolled her eyes at her butler. "Once
Hatchet got that telegram, he had me bundled up, packed
and headin' for London faster than an avalanche in the
Colorado Rockies. We got out of Lord Lovan's so quickly,
I don't think the man will ever speak to me again."

"Nonsense, madam," Hatchet said briskly; he pulled a
chair out for his employer. "Lord Lovan won't even notice

we're gone. It was a house party, you see," he explained to the others. "Even if he does notice our absence, I don't think he'll take umbrage at our hasty departure."

"Hasty departure," Luty snorted. "You didn't even let me finish my breakfast yesterday morning before you had me on the move." She plopped down in the chair and grinned. "But enough about that. Tell us who's been murdered."

"Pour yourselves some tea first," Mrs. Goodge said briskly. "And I'll get some more bread and butter. If you've been traveling, you'll be hungry."

"I'll get it," Betsy said, rising to her feet.

Mrs. Jeffries waited until the new arrivals had their refreshments before she began telling them about their latest case.

Luty and Hatchet listened carefully. When Mrs. Jeffries had finished, Luty put down her teacup and shook her head. "Not much to go on, is there?"

"Really, madam," Hatchet said quickly. "I think the household has done a rather good job of it so far. But I am confused as to why the inspector is being so close-mouthed."

" 'E's listenin' to his inner voice," Wiggins said. "Whatever that means."

Mrs. Jeffries didn't really want to take the time to explain what it meant. She felt just a bit foolish. After all, she was the one who'd told the inspector on more than one occasion to listen to his instincts, his inner voice and his guiding force. But goodness, she'd only said those things to keep the inspector's spirits up when he was feeling inadequate to the task at hand. She hadn't meant for him to take her literally. "Let's not worry about the inspector's reticence right now," she said briskly. "We've quite enough information to start with."

"Would you like me to have a word with these here fellows from Bestal's Brewery?" Luty asked. "I know a few people in the business; I reckon I can get something out of them."

"Madam," Hatchet said, "you own rather a lot of shares in some breweries, but I don't think that means you can go waltzing into this Mr. Pump or Mr. Magil's office and demand to know what they were doing at the Gilded Lily Pub."

"Don't be a pumpkinhead, Hatchet," Luty said irritably. "I can be subtle. And I can find out plenty too."

"I think you ought to 'ave a go at it," Smythe said, giving the elderly woman a cheeky grin. "We ain't been 'aving much luck ourselves."

"Thank you," Luty said graciously. "It's nice to know that someone around here thinks I know how to behave myself."

"Mrs. Jeffries," Hatchet said thoughtfully, "what would you like me to do?"

Mrs. Jeffries wasn't sure. "Why don't you see if you can find out anything about Tom and Joanne Dapeers. But it might be difficult for you, they don't have a lot of servants—"

"But they've got a lot of workers," Smythe interrupted. "They do own three pubs. I've only had a chance to work the Black Horse. Hatchet could dig around at the other two and see what he can find out." He looked at the butler. "The Dapeerses own the Horse and Trumpet over on Curzon Street and the White Boar just off Charing Cross Road."

Hatchet smiled gratefully. "Good, I'll go round today and see what I can dig up."

"I thought I'd have a go at finding out a bit more about Sarah Hewett," Betsy said casually. She didn't remind them that she was also planning to meet Hamilton and his sister at a pub later this afternoon. She wasn't sure that anyone, especially Smythe, would approve. He hadn't said a word yesterday when she'd mentioned Hamilton's name, but she'd seen the quick frown that crossed his face. Only a few months ago she wouldn't have cared whether or not something she did annoyed the coachman, but things had changed between the two of them. Betsy didn't want Smythe fretting.

"I think that's an excellent idea," Mrs. Jeffries said. "What are you going to be doing today, Smythe?" she asked, turning to the coachman.

"I thought I'd have another word with Molly and Mick; they was tendin' the bar that night at the Gilded Lily. They must know something. After that, I thought I'd try trackin' down the cabbie and the drayman that 'ad the dustup out in the street."

"Why do you want to talk to them?" Betsy asked curiously. "If they was fightin', neither of them could have seen anything."

"Maybe," Smythe admitted slowly, "and maybe not." He didn't want to tell them what he was really going to be up to today. It was too humiliating. Besides, he couldn't think of anything else to do. Thanks to Inspector Witherspoon shuttin' up tighter than the bloomin' Bank of England on Christmas Day, Smythe didn't have any idea of where this case was goin' or even who the real suspects were. He thought the others felt exactly the same way; they was just runnin' around in circles but they were too proud to admit it.

"That sounds very interesting, Smythe. I'm sure you'll find out all sorts of things." Mrs. Jeffries smiled cheerfully, delighted that the staff wasn't losing its enthusiasm.

Wiggins sighed. "I reckon you want me to 'ead back

over to the Gilded Lily and see what I can find out from the locals.''

Mrs. Jeffries gazed at the footman sympathetically. ''Do you feel up to it?''

He felt like crawling back into bed and pulling the covers over his head, but he'd never admit it in front of the others. '' 'Corse I do. I wasn't drunk, you know. Just a bit off-color—''

''Drunk!'' Luty exclaimed. ''Good Lord, Wiggins, have you taken to drinking yer troubles away?''

''It weren't my fault,'' the footman cried. ''The only way I could get anyone to talk to me was to buy 'em beer. Cost me a pretty penny, it did.''

''Gracious, Wiggins,'' Mrs. Jeffries said earnestly. ''No one expects you to do that.''

He was immediately ashamed of his outburst. He hadn't spent all that much yesterday. ''It's all right. I don't mind. Besides, I've got a bit tucked away. It's not like I have all that much to spend me coins on anyway.''

''Mind you don't overindulge yourself today,'' Mrs. Goodge said sharply. ''You don't have the constitution for it.''

Mrs. Jeffries silently debated whether or not to continue cautioning Wiggins about his money, but one look at his face convinced her that anything else said on the subject would just embarrass the lad. He, like everyone else in the household, was devoted to the inspector. She turned to the cook and asked, ''And what will you be doing today?''

''I've got some sources coming by,'' she replied. ''And I ought to pick up something. I put a few more queries out yesterday, so if I'm lucky, I'll hear a tidbit or two. But I must say, it's not easy picking up gossip about a publican.''

*   *   *

The inspector stood in the public bar of the Gilded Lily Pub and slowly turned in a circle. The pub was closed, of course, and likely to remain so for some time. Witherspoon thought it rather a shame. The place certainly was lovely.

"What are you doing, sir?" Constable Barnes asked.

"I'm trying to get a feel for the place," Witherspoon replied. Drat, his inner voice seemed to have gone to sleep. It wasn't telling him a thing. "Sometimes, one picks up all sorts of information just by being very observant," he said hastily, when he realized his constable was staring at him. "Er, is the barman here yet?"

"He's in the taproom. Mrs. Dapeers has instructed him to make an accounting of all the stock they have on hand."

"Really?" Witherspoon was surprised. "Is she going to open it up again?"

"I don't think so, sir. I believe she's probably going to sell out to her brother-in-law."

Witherspoon blinked in surprise. "How did you find that out?"

Barnes smiled slowly. "From Mrs. Tom Dapeers. She didn't tell me herself, sir. But I've worked with you long enough to pick up a few of your methods." He chuckled. "Excellent, they are, sir. You could give instruction to some of our other inspectors, that's what I say."

"Thank you, Constable." Witherspoon beamed proudly, though he hadn't a clue as to which of his "methods" the constable was referring to. "That's most kind of you. Do go on, tell me how you found out."

"Well, sir, Tessie Gainway—she's the barmaid at the Black Horse—she cornered me yesterday to tell me that one of the other barmaids, a woman named Ellen Hoxton, hadn't been around the neighborhood in a few days and her friends was gettin' worried."

"You mean someone's gone missing?"

"Oh no, sir." Barnes waved his hand in the air. "After I talked to Tessie for a few minutes, it become obvious the missing woman wasn't really missing at all. She'd been sacked from the Black Horse. She'd probably taken off to another part of London to look for work. It's quite a common occurrence. She wouldn't get another position around here if she'd been sacked, would she? But anyway, the important thing is that while Tessie and I were chattin' she happened to mention she'd overheard Mrs. Tom telling her husband that Moira Dapeers was going to sell out to them."

"Hmmm." Witherspoon still couldn't see which of his methods the constable had used, but he wasn't going to ask. "That's rather important information, Constable. I wonder if it means that Mrs. Tom has already spoken to Mrs. Dapeers about the property?"

"I don't know, sir," Barnes admitted. "But I think it's worth pursuing, don't you?"

"Indeed I do."

"You wanted to see me, Inspector," Mick called from the doorway. He wiped his big hands on the apron tied around his waist and came to stand behind the bar.

Witherspoon walked over to the bar. "Yes. Would you tell us what happened on the night of the murder?"

"What do ya mean?" Mick looked puzzled. "Mr. Dapeers walked into the taproom and someone shoved a knife in his back."

"No, no, that's not what I mean," Witherspoon said patiently. "What I really meant to ask was, could you tell us everything that happened from the time you came on duty until the murder."

Mick shoved a lock of dark hair off his broad forehead. "Well, I come in that mornin' about ten. Mr. Dapeers wanted us 'ere early because there was so much to do to get the place ready. The workmen were finishin' up in the back—''

"Workmen? What workmen?" No one told Witherspoon there had been workmen at the pub that day.

"The carpenters," Mick explained. "They was 'ere to fix that back door. It wouldn't close right. Mr. Dapeers was fit to be tied too. Kept on at 'em about how 'e'd paid a ruddy fortune to the builders and they'd damned well better have that back door fixed properly by openin' time." He broke off and laughed. " 'Corse they didn't pay 'im any mind. Just planed off the side of the door and stuck a bolt on the inside. But they had it fixed right by opening. I checked it myself. It locked, all right, but the hole for the bolt was big as yer fist and a two-year-old could probably toggle it open, if you know what I mean."

"And then what happened?" Witherspoon asked. Perhaps he shouldn't have asked Mick to tell him about the entire day. At this rate, he'd be standing here for hours.

"Then I went about my business, cleaning up, getting the bar stocked, you know, things like that."

The inspector nodded. "Was Mr. Dapeers here the entire day?"

"Most of it," Mick replied.

"Did anyone out of the ordinary come by?"

"Nah." Mick paused, his broad face creased in a puzzled frown. "Well, there was something, but it weren't so odd. . . ."

"What was it?"

"Ellen Hoxton, she was the barmaid at the Black Horse, she come round and wanted to see Mr. Dapeers."

"Did she see him?" Barnes asked.

"No, he'd stepped out for a minute, gone over to the bank, I think, so Ellen left Mr. Dapeers a note. I think she give it to Moll'."

"As I said, sir," Barnes said softly, "she was probably asking to see him to see if there was a position open here. Surprising, though. I'd have thought she'd have gone elsewhere in London to look for work."

"I expect she came here because she knew there was bad feeling between the Dapeers brothers," Witherspoon replied. "Possibly she thought that Haydon Dapeers would be sympathetic to someone who'd been sacked by his brother."

"Ellen were sacked by Mrs. Joanne," Mick put in quickly. "She's got a mouth on 'er, does Ellen. Sassed Mrs. Joanne once too often."

Too bad that Haydon Dapeers hadn't sacked the woman, Witherspoon thought. A disgruntled employee was often a good murder suspect. Then he was immediately ashamed of himself for making assumptions that weren't based on fact. Gracious, if every sacked employee in London killed someone, the streets would be littered with corpses. "Is Molly here this morning?"

Mick shook his head. "No. Since the murder, there's been no reason for her to come. There's nothing for her to do."

Witherspoon turned to Barnes. "Could you nip out and have one of the uniformed lads go get Molly. I think it's important that we speak with her." He also made a mental note to talk to Joanne Dapeers again.

"What time did you start letting people in the pub?" he asked Mick as soon as the constable had gone.

Mick scratched his head. "I dunno, I reckon it would have been about five o'clock."

"And how many people came in when you opened the doors?"

"About a dozen," Mick said. " 'Corse, most of them was here 'cause they'd been invited special."

"Could you tell me what happened right before Mr. Dapeers was murdered?" Witherspoon asked. He generally encouraged people to ramble on; it was amazing how much information one could pick up that way. But gracious, if Mick didn't get cracking with a few facts, he'd be here all day.

"I thought I was tellin' you," Mick replied.

"Yes, yes, of course you are, please go on."

"Well, let me see. Right before the murder you say." Mick scratched his head again, as though the event had taken place years ago. "Mr. Dapeers was talkin' to that dirty little man at the bar and then Molly told him that we needed another keg of beer. So he yelled back that he'd get it—Mr. Dapeers was the only one with a key to the taproom, you see. Then he walked down the hall and went inside. 'Bout the time he did that, the ruckus started out on the street and we all went over to have us a look. Most of us was still gawkin' at the fight when we heard Mrs. Joanne Dapeers screamin' her head off."

"How much time had passed between Mr. Dapeers going to the taproom and Mrs. Joanne Dapeers finding the body?" Witherspoon asked.

Mick shrugged. "I couldn't say, a few minutes maybe. No more than that. The copper had just got here to break up the fight when Mrs. Joanne found him. And it were a good fight, too. Two or three minutes of insults and shoutin' and then the fisticuffs started."

"The dirty little man that Dapeers had been talking to at the bar," Witherspoon asked. "Was he here during the fight?"

"I dunno. I think he'd left."

"Did you see him leave?"

"Nah." Mick wrinkled his nose. "But I wasn't watchin' the bloke, if you know what I mean."

"Do you know who he was?" the inspector asked.

"No, but I've seen him here before. He come around a couple of times and talked to Mr. Dapeers. They was doin' some kind of business together."

"Really?" Good, the inspector thought. Now they were getting somewhere.

" 'Corse they was," Mick said importantly. "He certainly weren't one of Mr. Dapeers's friends."

Smythe shifted his weight on the small, hard bench, trying to get comfortable. But it was a futile task. The Dirty Duck Pub was ancient, creaking and jammed up smack against the Thames. The place was dark, crowded and filled with the scent of unwashed bodies and stale beer. But the place had its advantages. Mainly, that it was Blimpey Groggins's local.

Smythe ignored the bold smile of the young woman at the next table. She was a streetwalker, tired looking, desperate, and probably with just enough money for a cheap gin before the barman tossed her out onto the docks. He felt sorry for women like her; there were plenty of them in this part of London.

He kept his gaze on the door, hoping that Blimpey would show up soon. If he didn't, Smythe's backside might be permanently ruined from this ruddy bench.

He hadn't told the others about Blimpey being in the Gilded Lily Pub on the night of the murder. Mainly because he hadn't known for sure it was Blimpey until just a few hours ago.

The front door opened. Smythe grinned. His prey had arrived. Blimpey strolled to the bar like he owned the place, which Smythe thought wasn't an impossibility, and ordered a beer. Then he turned to survey the room.

His eyes widened as he spotted the coachman. "What

you doin' 'ere?'' Blimpey asked as he sauntered over to where Smythe sat and plopped down on the opposite bench. "Waitin' to see me?"

"I didn't come 'ere for the beer," Smythe grimaced. "That's for sure. I want to ask you a few questions." He'd used Blimpey Groggins a time or two himself in the past on some of the inspector's other cases. Of course, Blimpey didn't know he was "helping the police with their inquiries," he was just doing what he always did, selling information for money. Luckily, Smythe had plenty of money.

"Questions? Me?" Blimpey chuckled. "Come on, mate. You know I don't do much talkin' unless me palm is crossed with silver."

Smythe stared at him. "You do a job for a fellow named Dapeers?"

Blimpey lifted his hands and rubbed his fingers together. "You're not playin' fair, Smythe. I don't see any lolly on the table."

Smythe sighed, pulled a few coins out of his pocket and slapped them down next to his glass. "There, 'appy now? Answer the question."

Blimpey's eyes shone greedily. "Now, that's more like it, mate. Yeah, I was doin' a job for a fellow named Dapeers." He snorted. "And it looks like I got paid just in time. Bloke got 'imself stabbed the other evening."

"What kind of a job was you doin'?"

"Took a message or two to a bloke for 'im, that's all." Blimpey stared at him cautiously, as though he'd just remembered that someone had been murdered and that Smythe worked for a Scotland Yard police inspector. "I didn't do all that much."

"What's the bloke's name?"

Blimpey hesitated, his gaze on the few coins under Smythe's fingertips. "Why are you so interested?"

"Never mind that. I'm payin' for information, so give it over."

"You're not thinkin' that I 'ad anything to do with killin' Dapeers, are ya?"

"Don't be daft," Smythe said. He'd known Blimpey for years. "You're not exactly as pure as snow, Blimpey, but you're no killer. Come on now, just give me the fellow's name."

Relieved, Blimpey grinned. "Name's McNally, James McNally."

"And what kind of messages was you takin' to this Mr. McNally?"

Blimpey took a long swallow of beer. "He owed Dapeers money. I was puttin' a bit of pressure on 'im, that's all."

"What kinda pressure?" Smythe asked suspiciously.

"I wasn't threatenin' the bloke," Blimpey protested. "I don't do that kinda work. All I did was tell McNally that Haydon Dapeers was gettin' tired of waitin' for his money. That's all."

"Why did McNally owe Dapeers money?"

Blimpey sighed dramatically and jerked his chin at the coins. "Is that all there is?"

"Maybe." Smythe grinned. "Why? You think your information is worth more than this?"

"Could be. Especially as Mr. McNally might be the kind of man who wouldn't want the world to know what he was up to."

Smythe silently debated. Finally, he reached into his pocket and pulled out a small roll of bills. Peeling a fiver off, he put it on the table next to the coins.

Blimpey reached for it; Smythe slapped his hand over the cash. "Not so fast; you 'aven't told me anything useful yet."

Frowning, Blimpey drew back. "All right, all right, you know I'm good for it. Haydon Dapeers was playin' the bookie for this McNally. McNally couldn't cover a couple of big bets, so Dapeers covered 'em for 'im. McNally's been slow payin' Dapeers back, so he sent me round to tell 'im to pay up or 'e'd be sorry."

"'Ow sorry?" Smythe asked. He wasn't surprised. A number of publicans in London did bookmaking on the side. But considerin' how the Gilded Lily looked, he wouldn't have figured Dapeers for one of them.

Blimpey shrugged. "You know I never ask those kinda questions, Smythe. I just took the message along to the fellow's office." He laughed merrily. "Bloke just about 'ad a stroke when the likes of me come through his front door. Couldn't get rid of me fast enough."

"What kind of offices? Where's it at?"

"Solicitor. Office is over on Curzon Street. Nice place, very posh, if you know what I mean."

Smythe picked up his beer and took a quick swallow. "Did he agree to pay Dapeers what he owed?"

"He said he would, but I didn't much believe 'im." Blimpey shook his head. "Bloke was skint. You can always tell. Claimed 'e'd go round that evening and straighten things out with Dapeers."

"Which evening?"

"The night of the murder, of course." Blimpey tapped the side of his now empty glass. "Care for another round?"

Smythe shuddered and pushed his half-full tankard away. "You go ahead."

"Another round over 'ere, guv," Blimpey yelled at the barman. "Anyways, like I was sayin', McNally said he'd go round that night to Dapeers's new pub and pay up. That's what I told Dapeers."

"So Dapeers was expectin' him to come by?"

"I think so. Mind you, we didn't have much time to talk about it. Dapeers went into the taproom and never come out."

"Did you see anything?"

"Nah." He broke off as the barmaid slapped his drink in front of him. "Ta, luv," he said, reaching for his beer. "I wasn't goin' to wait around for Dapeers. Didn't much like that pub and I'd told him what I'd come to say. I left right after that."

" 'Ad the street fight started when you left?"

"I 'eard some shoutin' as I was leavin', but I was in a 'urry so I didn't bother to stop and have a look-see." Blimpey shrugged. In his world, street fights were as common as muck. It would practically take a riot to get him to stop and pay attention. "Besides, I went out the door of the saloon bar. That comes out on Bonham Road; the ruckus was round the corner. Mind you, I was a bit surprised when I left."

"Why?"

" 'Cause I saw McNally walking down Bonham Road as I was going out."

Smythe sat up straighter. "McNally was there that night?"

"Well, I don't know if 'e was in the Gilded Lily"— Blimpey wiped his mouth on the greasy cuff of his jacket— "but I saw 'im skitterin' down Bonham Lane and then duckin' into the mews behind the Gilded Lily. Can't think why else some like 'im would be skulkin' about unless'n 'e were plannin' on payin' a visit to Dapeers."

" 'Ave you told the police about this?" Smythe asked, and then immediately knew it was a stupid question.

Blimpey threw back his head and laughed. "Cor, guv, remember who you talkin' to! The peelers and I have a mutual understandin'. I don't bother them and they don't bother me.''

Smythe studied Blimpey carefully. This was something the inspector should know about. Blast a Spaniard anyway, the only way Blimpey Groggins would ever walk into a police station and loosen his tongue would be if Smythe was holdin' a pistol to his back. Either that, or he'd have to pay the little crook a pretty penny. But maybe there was another way to get the information to the inspector. Smythe thought about it for a split second. ''I don't suppose you'd be willin' to tell the peelers about McNally?''

Blimpey's expression sobered. ''You suppose right. Look, Smythe, I make me livin' doin' jobs like this. Carryin' messages and findin' out things for people. People who trust me to keep me mouth shut. I go runnin' to the peelers and runnin' my trap about me tryin' to collect for a bookie and my business'll be ruined.'' He shook his head vehemently. ''You're a decent bloke and all that, and if I could do you a favor, I would. But I ain't goin' to run tattlin' to Scotland Yard about this. I've got me good name to consider, you know.''

Smythe stared at him for a long moment. The awful part was, he understood Blimpey's problem. Despite what the good, moral, upstanding citizens of London might think about collecting for bookmakers and running petty-ante gambling games, which Blimpey excelled at, people like him didn't have many choices in life. Poor, uneducated and usually hungry, they did what they had to do to survive. ''All right, Blimpey, you've made your point. Where does this McNally live?''

Betsy's conscience nagged her at her like a sore tooth. But she gamely pushed it aside. It wasn't her fault this poor boy actually thought she was interested in him. So inter-

ested, in fact, that he must have spent half the night talking
to his sister about the Dapeers household. She'd been surprised when she'd arrived at the pub to find him there
alone. But he'd explained that Sadie had come down with
a sore throat and couldn't come. Betsy didn't believe that
for a moment. She wasn't conceited, but a two-year-old
could work out that the poor lad wanted to be alone with
her. Now she felt lower than a snake. Once she found out
what she needed to know, she had no plans ever to see him
again. Stop it, she told herself fiercely. A murder's been
committed. She had to do what she had to do. "Oh Hamilton," she gushed. "I think it's ever so clever of you to
know so much about the Dapeers household. You must be
very observant."

"No." He blushed to the roots of his curly hair. "I'm
just a good listener. Most of what I know, my sister Sadie
told me. Like I said, Sadie worked there for a few months.
But then she got a chance for a better position in a milli-
ner's shop. It paid more and the hours is better, so she left
the Dapeers house. She didn't much like workin' there anyway, it weren't at all a nice place."

"Did they do a lot of arguin' and such?" Betsy asked.
She leaned closer across the small table.

"Nah," Hamilton replied. "It were mainly just the kind
of feelin' you get about a place that she didn't care for.
Said that Mr. Dapeers was always watchin' Mrs. Hewett
whenever he thought his wife wasn't looking. And poor
Mrs. Hewett went around with a long face and lookin' miserable all the time. The only time she ever smiled was when
she was with her daughter. She spent the rest of her time
hiding from Mr. Dapeers."

"How awful."

"It was. Sadie overheard a dreadful row the night before
she left." He glanced at her empty glass.

"Between Mr. Dapeers and Mrs. Hewett?" Betsy pressed.

"Would you like another ale?"

"No, thank you."

Hamilton picked up his beer and swallowed hastily. "It was between Mr. and Mrs. Dapeers. Seems that Mr. Dapeers didn't like his wife givin' so much time and money to Reverend Ballantine."

"Reverend Ballantine? Who is he?"

"He runs some kind of missionary society," Hamilton explained. "And Mr. Dapeers was right angry about Mrs. Dapeers giving him so much money."

Disappointed, Betsy slumped back in her chair. "Oh. Well, I guess there's lots of husbands who wouldn't want their wives giving away the household money."

Hamilton grinned and shook his head. "It weren't the household money she was giving away." He laughed. "Sadie said she heard Mrs. Dapeers shouting that it was her money she was using and she'd give it to whoever she liked."

Betsy brightened. "Mrs. Dapeers had money?"

"Pots of it, accordin' to Sadie," Hamilton said. "Mind you, most of it is tied up in some kind of trust, that's why Mr. Dapeers don't have control of it. They argued about that lots of times. He was always wantin' her to hire a solicitor and take some old relative of hers to court. But she refused to do it."

"So she gives this Reverend Ballantine money and tells her husband to mind his own business," Betsy murmured.

"If you ask me, Mr. Dapeers had a right to be angry," Hamilton said quickly. "It's not right, a wife having her own money."

Betsy's chin jerked up and she opened her mouth to tell him he was a ruddy fool. Women should have their own money! Then she remembered that she needed this young man to keep feeding her information, so she clamped down the angry retort on the tip of her tongue and forced herself to say, ''I think you're absolutely right.'' The words almost choked her; when she got home, she ought to wash her mouth out with soap.

Hamilton beamed at her, then he leaned forward and whispered, ''And that's not all Sadie heard, either. She heard Mr. Dapeers going on and on about how Mrs. Dapeers was making a fool of herself over this reverend.''

''You don't mean . . .''

''Yes,'' Hamilton whispered, ''I do mean.'' He glanced around the pub to make sure there were no ladies in earshot who might be offended by his next words. ''According to Sadie, Mr. Dapeers accused Mrs. Dapeers of carryin' on with the Reverend Ballantine. What's worse, the man is young enough to be her son.''

CHAPTER 5

Witherspoon was beginning to think his inner voice had gone mute. But no, he mustn't doubt himself. As his house-keeper always said, "You never give yourself enough credit, Inspector." He decided to be patient. Surely, this investigation would start making sense at some point.

He glanced at Barnes. The constable was staring out the window, his gaze fixed on the courtyard below. Barnes sniffed the air appreciatively, apparently enjoying the per-vasive scent of beer. They were in the offices of Bestal's Brewery.

"Did the clerk say he was going to go and get Mr. Pump?" Witherspoon inquired. "Seems we've been wait-ing an awful long time."

Barnes reluctantly turned away from the window. "It's only been a few minutes, sir."

"I'm dreadfully sorry to have kept you waiting," a voice said from the open doorway.

Startled, Witherspoon whirled about and saw a rather

plump gentleman with a full black beard advancing toward him.

The man extended his hand as he approached. "I'm Luther Pump," he said politely. "Mr. Magil will be along in a minute. He's out in the yard."

"I'm Inspector Witherspoon from Scotland Yard and this is Constable Barnes," The inspector replied as they shook hands.

"I know who you are. We saw you the other night when we were at the Gilded Lily. Do sit down, gentlemen." Pump waved at a couple of chairs in front of a huge desk. He went round behind the desk and sat down. "I know why you're here, and I must say, I don't think I can be of much help. Mr. Magil and I only met Mr. Dapeers that night. We were dreadfully shocked about what happened, of course. Dreadfully shocked."

"Naturally." Witherspoon smiled politely. "Murder is always very upsetting. Let me assure you, sir, we won't take much of your time. We've only a few routine questions to ask you."

"It may be routine to you, Inspector," Pump said. "But it's rather upsetting for me, I've never been involved in this sort of thing before. But do go on and make your inquiries."

"First of all," the inspector said slowly, "why were you at Mr. Dapeers's pub that evening?"

"He'd invited us to come round," Pump said. He hesitated. "Actually, he hadn't so much invited us as, well, this is most awkward. Perhaps I shouldn't say any more until Mr. Magil gets here. He's better at explaining this sort of thing than I am."

"I'm here now." Edward Magil strode into the room, dusting his hands off as he walked. "Good day, gentlemen," he said, pulling another chair up next to Pump's desk and quickly seating himself. "I'm Edward Magil."

"Yes, we assumed as much," Witherspoon replied. He glanced at Barnes to see if the constable had his notebook out. Barnes was already scribbling in it.

"I've just asked Mr. Pump why you were at the Gilded Lily on the night of the murder," the inspector said. "He seems a bit unsure—"

"We were at the Gilded Lily because Haydon Dapeers had written us a letter."

"A letter?"

"Yes," Magil said firmly. "A letter about a matter of grave concern to us."

Witherspoon straightened his spine. Now they were getting somewhere. Yes, indeed, he would finally start getting some answers. "Grave concern?" he echoed.

"Indeed," Magil replied. "Inspector, how much do you know about the pub business?"

Witherspoon blinked. He knew as much as any policeman about the licensing laws and those sorts of matters. What else was there to know? "Well, I think I'm as well-informed as—"

Magil waved his hand impatiently. "I'm sure you are," he interrupted, "but there are a few facts about our business that the general public doesn't understand. Did you know that breweries loan money to people who want to go into the pub business?"

Witherspoon didn't know that, but he was loath to admit it. "Er—"

"No, of course you don't. But that's what we do, you see. We loan money to people so they can go into the pub business, and in return, they have to sell our goods exclusively. We're quite particular about who we lend our money to, as well. One couldn't just hand out capital to any person who came along and wanted to open a public house, could one?''

"No, I suppose one couldn't," Witherspoon replied politely.

"Bestal's insists upon the very highest standards of integrity and character. Do you understand?''

"I think so.'' The inspector was dreadfully confused. What did all this have to do with anything? But he schooled himself to be patient.

"It's quite competitive, the beer business," Luther Pump interjected. "Beer consumption has fallen dreadfully in the last ten years. Those awful temperance lobbies have seen to that. Thank God the Conservatives are back in power. It's a wonder the Liberals didn't drive us all to the poorhouse.''

"I'm sure the inspector isn't interested in the political aspects of the brewery business, Luther," Magil said irritably.

As Witherspoon didn't have a clue what the Liberals or the Conservatives had to do with pubs and beer, he said nothing.

"But as I was saying," Magil continued, "we loan money to people to finance their pubs and we have very, very strict rules about that."

"And these rules are?"

Magil waved his hand dismissively. "Oh, most of them don't really matter, at least they had nothing to do with our visit to Haydon Dapeers. What is important is that Dapeers had contacted us telling us that he had information of grave concern to us.''

Witherspoon sighed silently. His inner voice was silent, his head hurt and the smell of this place was making him ill. "And what would that be, sir?''

Magil leaned forward, his expression as somber as a

vicar conducting a funeral. "I trust you keep what I'm going to tell you completely confidential."

"Er, I'm not sure I can give you that assurance, sir. This is a murder investigation, you know. Whatever you say to me can be used in evidence at a trial."

Magil glanced at his colleague.

Pump nodded almost imperceptibly. "We've got to tell them," he said. "It's far better for the inspector to know the truth now than to risk us having to testify to it in open court."

"But—" The inspector tried to tell them that even if they told him now, they might still have to testify in court.

But Magil wasn't listening to him. "You're right, of course," he said to his colleague.

He turned to the two policemen and leaned closer. Dropping his voice to a whisper, he said, "Haydon Dapeers implied the most awful thing. He said he had evidence that one of our pubs was watering down the beer."

Wiggins's feet hurt, his shirt collar was too tight and his stomach still felt queasy. He wished he were home sitting in the cool of the kitchen rather than hanging about on Bonham Road trying to find someone who knew something about the murder.

"You look peaked, boy," a woman's voice said from behind him.

Wiggins whirled around and saw a woman with blue eyes and dark brown hair smiling at him. She was dressed in a pale lavender dress and had a rather tatty white feather in her hair. At first glance he thought she must be in her thirties, but upon closer inspection he realized she was young, probably not more than a few years older than himself. "It's the sun," he murmured, feeling his cheeks starting to flame as he realized exactly what this woman was.

"I expect I ought to get inside and sit down."

Her smile turned coy. "I've got a room across the way." She jerked her chin toward a small, run-down-looking house across the road. "If you've a mind to, you can rest a bit there."

Wiggins didn't know what to do. So he did what he always did and opened his mouth without thinking. "Look, I don't 'ave any money. . . ."

She laughed. "I'm not drummin' up trade, boy. Just offerin' you a kindness. You're as white as a sheet and you look like you're about to faint."

"Sorry," he muttered, ashamed of himself and embarrassed to boot. Just because this woman was probably poor and made her living walking the streets didn't mean she couldn't be kind to a stranger. "But I thought you was . . ."

"I don't work durin' the daytime," the woman replied. "Look, there's a pub over there."

Wiggins groaned.

"Or," she continued cheerfully as she watched him clutch his stomach, "there's a coffeehouse round the corner; we can go there and get us a bite to eat. You look like you could use somethin' on yer stomach. And I do hate to eat alone."

Wiggins smiled sheepishly. In between the rolls of nausea, he was hungry. And thanks to an unknown generous benefactor at Upper Edmonton Gardens, he did have extra money. Because this mysterious person frequently gifted everybody in the household with small, useful presents, he'd been able to save virtually all his wages for the last two quarters. Patting his pocket, he said, "That sounds a right good idea. But please, I'd like to buy you something to eat. You've been so kind."

"That's ever so nice of you." She batted her eyelashes shamelessly and grinned. "The coffeehouse is just around here.'' Linking her arm in his, she hurried them both toward the corner.

As she hustled him into the coffeehouse and over to a table, Wiggins had a sneaking suspicion a free meal might have been her aim all along. He was wearing a brand-new white shirt and a new pair of shoes. He probably looked like an easy mark; his new clothes alone set him a cut above most of the working people round here. But as he had nothing better to do and he'd never been in a coffeehouse before, he didn't much mind.

''Will a ploughman's do you?'' she asked. He nodded. ''Two ploughman's over here and a glass of ale,'' she called to the waiter. ''Do you want one?''

As the very thought of beer made his stomach curdle, he shook his head. ''No thanks.''

''My name's Bronwen Jones,'' she said chattily, plopping her elbows on the table and grinning at him. ''What's yours?''

''I'm Wiggins.''

''Wiggins what?'' she asked. ''Ta,'' she said to the waiter as he put two plates of bread, pickled onions and cheese on the table in front of them.

Wiggins would die before he told anyone his first name. ''Just Wiggins.''

''You work round these parts?'' Bronwen asked. She stuffed a huge bite of bread in her mouth.

Wiggins hesitated. He could hardly tell her the truth, that he was over here snooping about finding clues to a murder. He decided to do the next best thing. She might be a local, she might know something. ''Not really.'' He gave her another sheepish grin. ''I guess you could say I just come over to these parts 'cause I 'eard about that murder. Curious, that's all. Thought I'd 'ave a gander at the pub.''

"You mean that publican that got himself stabbed." She snatched up the cheese.

"Right. Fellow named Haydon Dapeers."

Her eyes narrowed dangerously. "I know the bastard's name. And if someone shoved a knife in his back, good for them, I say."

Wiggins couldn't believe his luck. "You knew the man?"

"Everyone round 'ere knows 'im," she snorted. "And most don't like him much. Real pig, he is. Tryin' to run his own brother out of business. Not that Tom's all that much better than Haydon, but at least Tom and Joanne mind their own business and don't go callin' the law on us just for 'angin' about outside the pub to pick up a bit of trade."

"What do you mean," Wiggins asked, "about his brother-in-law?"

She swallowed her cheese. "Just what I said. Tom and Joanne 'ave worked right 'ard to make their pub a success. Not too many pubs on this street, that's why they come 'ere. And what does that bastard do, he opens one up just a few yards up the road from theirs. Done it deliberately, accordin' to my friend Ellen, and she ought to know: she used to work for Tom and Joanne."

"Who's Ellen?" Wiggins was getting confused and he knew he shouldn't because tonight when he met with the others after dinner, he'd have to give them all the facts.

"Ellen Hoxton. She's a friend of mine. Mind you, she doesn't work at the Black Horse anymore. She got sacked for sassin' Joanne. 'Ard one is Joanne. Real 'ard."

"And this Ellen claims that Dapeers deliberately opened his pub to drive his own brother out of business?" Wiggins hoped he sounded like just a nosey parker and not someone who was really trying to pick up information.

"That's what Ellen said. She said she overheard them havin' a right old row about it. Joanne and Tom was both furious." She broke off and nodded at Wiggins's plate. "You goin' to eat that cheese?"

He pushed his plate toward her. She needed this food a lot more than he did. "My stomach's still not right. You have it."

"Ta," she replied, pushing her empty plate to one side and yanking his over to take its place. "Anyways, like I was saying: Ellen overheard this terrible row. Tom and Haydon was goin' at each other like cats and dogs."

"Where could I find this Ellen?"

Bronwen stopped eating and gave him a long, speculative stare. "You're a curious one, aren't you?"

He wondered if he'd overplayed his hand. "Guess I am, at that. Mind you, you're bein' awful polite about it. Most people just tell me I'm nosy as sin."

She laughed. "No harm in that. Especially when it's something as juicy as murder."

"So where's this Ellen at?" he persisted. Bronwen had tucked back into the food with such relish he hoped she hadn't forgotten his question.

"Don't know." She shrugged. "Ain't seen Ellen since she got tossed out of the Black Horse."

"And when was that?"

"A day or two before Haydon got himself stabbed." She frowned slightly. "No, I tell a lie. I did see Ellen after that."

"Where?"

She grew thoughtful and put the last bite of cheese back down on her plate. "That's the funny part," she murmured. "Mind you, I didn't think anything of it at the time. Considerin' that Ellen didn't much like Haydon Dapeers and all."

"Yeah," Wiggins encouraged.

"The last time I saw Ellen, she was in the Gilded Lily Pub and she and Haydon were chattin' like they was old friends."

Mrs. Jeffries carefully looked up and down the street as she crossed the road to the Gilded Lily Pub. Even with her ability to talk her way out of awkward situations, considering the inspector's present state of mind, she didn't want to run into him just now.

She saw no one she recognized, only a police constable keeping watch on the corner. Smiling serenely and keeping her shopping basket tucked over her arm, she sauntered toward her goal. The Gilded Lily was closed, of course. But she slowed her pace and managed to get a good look in the window. Yet there wasn't much to see; the interior was too dark. Continuing on, she came to Bonham Road, turned the corner and tried looking in the window of the saloon bar. Same problem. Not near enough light to make anything out.

A few yards up the road, she spotted the entrance to the mews. Mrs. Jeffries cast a quick glance over her shoulder and headed that way. Within seconds she was standing outside the back door of the pub. Realizing it was probably foolish, she lifted her hand, grasped the knob and turned. To her amazement, the door swung open.

She hesitated, glanced to her left and right to make sure she wouldn't be seen and then slipped inside. Stepping softly, she made her way down the darkened hall. At the first door, she stopped, tried the handle and sighed in disappointment when it wouldn't budge.

But then she heard voices.

They were low-pitched and quiet, barely above a whisper. Mrs. Jeffries tiptoed quietly down the hall, stopping short of the opening that led to the saloon bar. The voices were louder now, but not clear enough for her to hear properly. She dropped to her knees, tucked her shopping basket out of the way, lifted her skirts and crawled closer to the opening leading to the public bar.

"I think we ought to leave London. I'd like to pack up and go and never come back." It was a woman's voice. Mrs. Jeffries desperately wanted to see who was speaking, but she didn't dare raise her head.

"But we haven't done anything," a man replied. "And I'll not have your name tainted with a murder charge. Not after all that you've endured in that house."

"The police were round. They asked me a lot of questions," she said.

"The police are questioning everyone," he said softly.

"But I hated Haydon," she cried. "And I was stupid enough to let that inspector know it."

"Everyone hated Haydon," he exclaimed. "You had nothing to do with his murder, though. So you've nothing to worry about."

"I've everything to worry about," she insisted, her voice catching. "I came back inside the pub that night. I was here when he was being killed. Someone probably saw me. I was standing right at the bar. Someone will remember, someone will tell the police they saw me go back inside before that stupid fight finished out on the street. They'll blame Haydon's murder on me."

"That's not going to happen," the man said. "I won't let it."

Mrs. Jeffries had to see who was speaking. She risked peeking around the door. In a dark corner of the bar, she could make out the two figures. Even in the dim light, she could see that the woman was young, blond and pretty. The man was dressed in a white shirt and dark trousers, his face half in shadow.

"But you won't be able to do anything about it," the woman said passionately.

"I've got money now," he replied, grasping her by the shoulders. "And if I have to, I'll spend every penny of it to protect you and the child."

Mrs. Jeffries's knees began to tingle. She wasn't as young as she used to be; she eased back, trying to get more comfortable while still keeping her vantage point. Unfortunately, as she moved, her foot connected with her shopping basket. A loud scratching noise cut through the quiet room as the wicker basket skittered backward. Mrs. Jeffries quickly ducked back behind the door. She glanced down the long hallway, wondering if she could make it to the door before she was discovered.

"What's that?" the woman asked.

The man let go of her and leapt to his feet. "Stay here," he ordered. "It may be the police."

Mrs. Jeffries debated about whether to try to make a dash for it. But she hesitated a moment too long.

The man's face appeared from around the doorway. "Who the devil are you?" he demanded.

"What time is Mrs. Jeffries expected back?" Betsy asked excitedly as she hurried into the kitchen. "I've got ever so much to tell everyone."

"She should have been back half an hour ago," Mrs. Goodge replied. She continued to lay out the tea things. "I expect she got held up and will be in at any moment."

"What about Wiggins and Smythe?" Betsy snatched up her apron from the back of the chair, tied it around her waist and picked up the tea tray Mrs. Goodge had sitting on the sideboard.

"They should be back soon too." The cook slapped a plate of buns on the table. "They know we're having a meeting this afternoon."

By the time the two women had finished setting the table, Wiggins and Smythe had both arrived home. But Mrs. Jeffries hadn't.

"How much longer do you think we ought to wait for her?" Betsy asked worriedly as she glanced at the kitchen clock. It wasn't like the housekeeper to be late. Especially for one of their meetings.

"I'm sure she'll be along any minute," Mrs. Goodge said, but she too looked concerned.

"Maybe we should start without 'er," Wiggins ventured. "I'd like to get back out and do a bit more snoopin'."

"We can't start without her," Betsy snapped. "It wouldn't be right."

"Well, I don't think she'd mind all that much," the footman said defensively. "We can always catch her up this evenin' after supper."

Betsy frowned. "I still don't think it's right—"

"I do," Smythe cut in quickly. "Mrs. Jeffries would be the first to tell us to carry on. Just because she's late is no reason for us to mope around 'ere twiddlin' our thumbs, not when we've a killer to catch."

"You're absolutely right, Smythe," Mrs. Jeffries said. They all turned and saw the housekeeper, out of breath and her tidy bonnet askew, rushing toward the table. "I'm so dreadfully sorry to be late, but I'm afraid it was unavoidable."

"What 'appened?" Smythe asked. "Are you all right?"

"I'm fine." She pulled out her chair at the head of the table and plopped down. "But a cup of tea would do nicely right now. I'm afraid I got caught snooping."

"Got caught," Wiggins cried. "By who? The inspector? Constable Barnes?"

"No, no, it wasn't as bad as all that." She waved her hand in the air. "But it wasn't the most pleasant experience I've ever had either."

"What 'appened?" Smythe asked.

Mrs. Jeffries took the cup of tea that Mrs. Goodge handed to her. "Well, I decided to have a look at the scene of the crime, so to speak—"

"You went round to the Gilded Lily?" Wiggins cried. "But that's daft—"

"Stop interruptin'," Betsy interrupted the footman, "and let Mrs. Jeffries finish."

"Thank you, Betsy." Mrs. Jeffries smiled at the maid. "And while I was there I discovered the back door was unlocked."

Smythe shook his head in disgust. "Ya didn't go in, did ya? Bloomin' Ada, Mrs. J, that *was* a daft thing to do."

"Possibly," she replied calmly, "but sometimes one has to take risks if one is to learn anything. And I do believe I learned rather a lot this afternoon."

"Go on," Mrs. Goodge encouraged, "tell us the rest of it."

"When I got inside, I heard voices coming from the public bar. Naturally, I was curious; the place was supposed to be closed. So I crept up the hall and listened. There were two people in the bar; obviously they were using the Gilded Lily as a meeting place because they assumed it would be safe from prying eyes. Well, unfortunately, I accidentally kicked my shopping basket; they heard the noise and the man came to investigate."

"Who were they?" Betsy asked.

"Michael Taggert and Sarah Hewett," Mrs. Jeffries said thoughtfully. "And once Mr. Taggert got over the shock of finding me, I must say he was quite a gentleman about the whole thing. Of course, I did have a bit of explaining to do.''

"What did you tell him?" Mrs. Goodge asked.

"The truth," Mrs. Jeffries replied calmly.

Their was a collective groan from around the table.

"Now, now," Mrs. Jeffries said quickly, "it's not as bad as all that. But I had to tell them something and it's rather difficult to think when one is on one's knees hiding behind a door."

"Exactly what did ya tell 'em?" Smythe asked.

"Just that I was the housekeeper to Inspector Gerald Witherspoon and that I occasionally helped out a bit with his investigations."

"So you didn't mention any of us?" Mrs. Goodge pressed.

Mrs. Jeffries hesitated. She knew what was worrying them. The number of people who knew the household helped the inspector with his murder cases seemed to be growing by leaps and bounds. It was a problem that concerned her as well. But sometimes one didn't have much choice in these matters. "As a matter of fact, I did."

There was another collective groan.

She ignored them and carried on. "The only way I could get Michael Taggert to believe me," she explained, "was to tell him everything. But don't worry, he's an artist."

"What's that got to do with anything?" Wiggins exclaimed.

"I mean, he's got rather a more open mind than most people," she said hurriedly. "And after I told him what we did, he was really quite forthcoming about everything. If you're worried that he or Mrs. Hewett are going to say anything to anyone, don't be. I think the both of them are rather good at keeping secrets."

"Mrs. Jeffries," Smythe said somberly. "We ain't nig-gled about that. But bloomin' Ada, this is a murder inves-tigation and you was trapped in a deserted pub by two of the suspects. Don't ya see what we're gettin' at? You coulda been killed. Either of them two could have been the murderer and they wouldn'a thought twice about stickin' a knife in your back."

She was suddenly rather ashamed of herself. Here she was thinking they were only concerned about more people learning their secret, while in reality, they'd been worried about her safety. "But that didn't happen," the house-keeper assured him quickly. "And furthermore, I don't think either of them is the killer. As a matter of fact, I'm sure of it."

"Don't be," Smythe retorted. " 'Cause I found out to-day that Michael Taggert didn't leave the Gilded Lily after his set-to with Dapeers. He come back around Bonham Road and slipped into the saloon bar. He was there when Dapeers was murdered."

"And Sarah Hewett's not exactly a grievin' young widow, either," Mrs. Goodge added. "Accordin' to my sources, there was no love lost between her husband and herself."

"And she hated Dapeers," Betsy interjected. "From what I learned today, she had as much reason to kill him as anyone else."

Mrs. Jeffries threw up her hands. "Listen, this isn't doing us a bit of good. Why don't we all calm down, tell one another what we've found out today and then try to sort things out calmly and rationally. Mrs. Goodge, you go first."

The cook looked as though she'd love nothing more than to continue lecturing the housekeeper on the folly of taking silly risks, but as she actually had something to report, she resisted the urge. "All right, then. First of all, like I was sayin', I found out that Sarah Hewett wasn't in love with her late husband."

"That don't make her a killer," Betsy said. "From what I can tell, half the women in London don't much care for their husbands."

"True," Mrs. Goodge replied. "But after her husband died, Sarah was stuck living in the Dapeers household. Seems she and Moira get along all right, but she hated Haydon Dapeers. Rumor has it that he couldn't keep his hands to himself, if you know what I mean. With him dead, Sarah can breathe just a bit easier. And there was somethin' peculiar about the way she up and married Charles Hewett—poor fellow had been in love with her for a long while and she wouldn't give him the time of day. Then all of a sudden she throws herself at him and they elope."

"Why'd she live there if she 'ated Dapeers so much?" Wiggins asked curiously.

"She probably didn't have any choice, her husband probably left her destitute," Betsy guessed.

"No." Mrs. Goodge shook her head. "He left her an annuity, at least that's what my sources told me, but for some reason, she decided to stay at the Dapeers house."

"That still isn't a motive for murder," Betsy complained. She was rather cross that the cook had found out one of the very things she was going to report.

"Did you learn anything else?" Mrs. Jeffries asked.

Mrs. Goodge shook her head. "Not really, except that Haydon Dapeers wasn't a very nice man. Quite a number of people disliked him."

"Includin' his own wife," Betsy interjected.

"Do go on, Betsy," Mrs. Jeffries encouraged.

"Well, I met Hamilton at the pub this afternoon," she began.

Smythe's brows drew together in a quick frown. "You went to a pub with a stranger?"

"Hamilton isn't a stranger. I met him yesterday."

"Where?" Smythe persisted. Bloomin' Ada, did every female in this household take it into their heads to do something daft and dangerous today?

"He's the lad that works in the grocer's around the corner from the Dapeers house," she explained. "His sister used to work for Haydon and Moira Dapeers. That's why I wanted to talk to him."

Smythe still wasn't happy. "Was 'is sister there today?"

"No," Betsy said irritably. "She wasn't. But Hamilton knew plenty about the Dapeers household and he told me everything."

Mrs. Jeffries could see that Smythe didn't like hearing that Betsy had spent part of her day at a pub with a young man. The maid and the coachman were tentatively finding their way into a courtship. "How very clever of you, Betsy," she said quickly.

Betsy smiled broadly and went on to tell them everything else she'd found out. When she was finished, Mrs. Jeffries nodded approvingly and then turned to Smythe. "Did you learn much today?"

Smythe shrugged. "A bit. Seems that Haydon Dapeers was runnin' a gamblin' game on the side. Actin' as bookmaker to a few select customers. The one that I'm most interested in is a solictor named James McNally." He supplied them with the details he'd picked up from Blimpey Groggins. "I thought I'd see what I could find out about McNally this evening, seems to me 'e's got to be considered a suspect. 'E was there."

"I think that's a splendid idea," Mrs. Jeffries agreed.

"And I thought I'd see what else I could learn about

Moira Dapeers and Reverend Ballantine," Betsy put in, not wanting to be outdone by the coachman.

"Excellent, Betsy," Mrs. Jeffries replied. She turned her attention to Wiggins. "And how did you fare today?"

Wiggins squirmed uncomfortably. He wasn't at all certain how to tell them the only person he'd talked with was a . . . he couldn't bring himself to even think of the word commonly used to describe Bronwen's occupation. He'd liked her. She was a nice person, despite what she had to do for a living. "Oh, I did all right."

He decided to just tell them his information without mentioning who he'd acquired it from. "I found out that Tom and Joanne Dapeers really 'ated Haydon. They thought 'e'd opened the Gilded Lily deliberately on the same street that they was on just to run 'em out of business. Haydon Dapeers 'ad tried to do that before, you know. When they opened one of their other pubs, Haydon had up and opened the Pale Swan just up the road from 'em."

"Do you know that for a fact or is your source just guessing?" Mrs. Jeffries asked.

"She seemed to know what she was on about," Wiggins replied. "And what's more, one of the barmaids from the Black Horse, she got sacked for sassin' Mrs. Joanne Dapeers, she was seen 'angin' about the Gilded Lily the day before the murder or maybe it was the mornin' of the murder, Bronwen weren't sure. But she's disappeared."

They all stared at him. He wasn't making a lot of sense. Finally, Mrs. Jeffries said, "I'm afraid I'm not following you. Does this person have anything to do with Dapeers's murder?"

"Who were you talkin' to today?" Smythe asked.

"What's a sacked barmaid from the Black Horse got to do with the murder at the Gilded Lily?" Betsy exclaimed.

"Wiggins, has this heat addled your brain?" Mrs. Goodge charged.

"Wiggins," Mrs. Jeffries said gently. "Why don't you start over. Start at the beginning and tell us everything."

CHAPTER 6

⸺⸺

"It's been a rather tiring day," the inspector said to Mrs. Jeffries as he followed her into the drawing room. "A nice glass of sherry will be just the very thing I need."

"I'll pour you one, sir," she replied, "sit yourself down and get comfortable. You can tell me all about your grueling day." Mrs. Jeffries sincerely hoped the inspector had got over being so tight-lipped about this case. Everyone in the household had learned something today. It was imperative that she get the inspector investigating a few of the clues the staff had turned up. Not that she could actually come right out and *tell* him, of course. But if she could get him talking, she had her ways of getting the information across.

"Oh, I don't think I want to talk about the case," Witherspoon said, waving his hand in the air dismissively. "As you've often told me, Mrs. Jeffries, sometimes it's best just to let all the information one learns stew about in one's mind until it's done."

Mrs. Jeffries almost dropped the decanter of sherry. Goodness, what was she going to do now? Who would have thought the inspector would have taken her casual words of encouragement when he was doubting his abilities as a policeman so very seriously. She could hardly insist he talk about the murder. But if he didn't, how was she going to get him thinking about Moira Dapeers and the Reverend Ballantine, or Ellen Hoxton, the barmaid sacked from the Black Horse, or James McNally? In the future, she vowed as she used her apron to wipe up the drops of sherry she'd spilled on the sideboard, she'd be more careful in what she said to the man. Apparently he took her words far more seriously than expected. But she refused to give up. As Luty Belle sometimes said, there's more than one way to skin a cat.

"I think that's a marvelous idea, sir," she said cheerfully. "When you're home, you ought to be relaxing, not thinking about an insoluble murder."

"Insoluble?" he echoed, his eyebrows raising above his spectacles.

"Oh dear." She handed him a glass of sherry. "Pardon me, sir. I didn't mean to use that word."

"Gracious, I should hope not," he replied. "Why you've told me yourself, no case is insoluble."

"I didn't mean that quite the way it sounded, sir," she said quickly, feeling like a worm at the terrified expression that had flitted across Witherspoon's face. "What I meant to say was that the case was difficult, not insoluable."

"I should hope so, Mrs. Jeffries." He sank back in his seat and reached for his sherry. "I like to believe that justice will always prevail. It may take me a while, but I do think that eventually I'll catch the culprit."

He sounded as though he were trying to convince himself, not her. "Of course you will, sir," she replied.

"I'll admit this case is, as you say, difficult. But gracious, you've told me dozens of times that no crime is impossible to solve."

"I've absolute faith in your abilities, Inspector," she said. "Eventually, you will catch this killer. I've no doubt of it."

Witherspoon said nothing for a moment. He took a sip of sherry and regarded her steadily over the rim of his glass. "You know, I think perhaps I ought to talk about the case. Get the ideas flowing, that sort of thing."

"If you'd like to, sir," she said casually, as though the matter was of no consequence. "I do so enjoy hearing all the fascinating details of your methods. They're so very, very brilliant." She wondered if perhaps she wasn't piling it on a bit thick.

"You're far too kind, Mrs. Jeffries," he said.

"Did you learn anything useful today, sir?" she asked quickly. She felt rather bad. From the expression on the poor man's face, she knew she'd seriously undermined his self-confidence. Drat. But she'd had to do something.

"I'm not sure." Witherspoon frowned. "Sometimes one isn't, you know. Sometimes one doesn't know whether what one has learned has any connection to the crime, or whether one is just chasing one's tail. Take today, for instance. Constable Barnes and I went round and had a chat with the gentlemen from the Bestal's Brewery. They were at the Gilded Lily the night of the murder."

"And were they able to tell you anything useful?" she asked.

Witherspoon's brows drew together as his spectacles slipped down his nose a notch. "Not really." He sighed dramatically. "Neither of them actually knew the victim. They'd only gone to the Gilded Lily in response to a letter that Dapeers had sent them."

"What kind of letter?" she asked curiously.

He smiled faintly. "It seems they were concerned that someone was watering down their beer. Breweries apparently don't like that sort of thing. Gives them a bad name in the business."

Mrs. Jeffries was somewhat disappointed. She'd hoped for something a bit more interesting than this petty nonsense. Watered beer, indeed. "Did they see anything while they were there?" she pressed. She wanted to get as many facts as possible out of Witherspoon. In his current state of mind, he might dry up rather quickly. Besides, there was always the chance that one of these gentlemen might have noticed some little something which could give them the clue they needed.

"No. Like everyone else, when the street ruckus started up, they dashed out to the front to have a look."

"I see," Mrs. Jeffries replied. "Did you talk to any of the other suspects today?"

Witherspoon started to reply when there was a loud banging on the front door. "I wonder who that can be at this time of the evening," he murmured.

Betsy's footsteps sounded in the hall. They heard the front door open and then close. A moment later Betsy came into the drawing room carrying a letter. "This is for you, sir," she said, handing it to him. "Mrs. Philpott just brought it round. It was delivered there by mistake this afternoon."

"Thank you, Betsy." Witherspoon tore the envelope open and yanked out the letter. He flipped to the last page and read the signature.

"It's from Lady Cannonberry," he cried happily.

Betsy and Mrs. Jeffries exchanged glances.

"How very nice, sir," the housekeeper said.

"I'll take it upstairs to read," he announced, leaping to

his feet. Clutching the letter to his chest, he hurried out of the room, pausing only long enough to say, "Call me when dinner is served."

"Drat," Mrs. Jeffries murmured as soon as he'd disappeared. "That was most unfortunate timing. I almost had him talking."

"Sorry," Betsy replied. "But I didn't think. When the letter came, I thought it might be something to do with the case."

"It wasn't your fault," Mrs. Jeffries said. "You didn't know who the letter was from or that he'd dash off like a schoolboy to read it in his room."

"Did you get anything out of him?"

"Not very much," Mrs. Jeffries admitted. "But I hope to do better after dinner. There's so much about this case the inspector doesn't know. I must find a way to tell him. I really must. We've made ever so much progress."

"Do you really think so?" Betsy asked doubtfully. "Seems to me we're all just dashin' about findin' things out that don't make any difference."

It seemed that way to Mrs. Jeffries as well, but she wasn't going to admit it to the maid. There was no point in the rest of the household being as depressed about this case as she was. It was important to keep their spirits up. "It may seem that way," she said firmly, "but believe me, every bit of information we gather is useful."

"What did Inspector Witherspoon tell you?"

"He didn't really have time to say much at all. Only that the gentlemen from Bestal's Brewery didn't really know the victim, hadn't seen a thing and are more concerned with someone watering down their beer than they are with a murder."

*   *   *

Despite the fact that she hadn't gotten another word about the case out of Inspector Witherspoon at dinner, Mrs. Jeffries was in quite good spirits the next morning.

She'd done quite a bit of thinking about the case before she went to bed and had decided that it was moving along nicely, even without the inspector's information. So far, there were any number of suspects who could have committed the crime.

She tied an apron around her waist and then put the kettle on to boil. It would be half an hour before the rest of the household roused. She wanted to have a nice quiet cup of tea and do some more thinking. She brewed herself a pot of tea, took it over to the table and sat down.

First of all, she thought, who had access to the taproom at the time of the murder? That was easy. Virtually everyone in the pub. Anyone could have slipped down that darkened hallway and stuck a knife in Haydon Dapeers's back. She paused, her cup halfway to her lips, as another thought struck her. The knife. Goodness, she was an idiot. She hadn't found out if the knife had been in the pub or if the killer brought it with them. She'd forgotten to follow up that clue and it was vitally important she do so. She made a mental note to pry that information out of the inspector at breakfast even if she had to use a crowbar!

And what of the two lovers she'd interrupted in the pub yesterday? It was obvious they'd decided to meet at the Gilded Lily because they didn't want to be seen. But why not? Sarah Hewett was respectfully widowed and Michael Taggert wasn't engaged or married. Why not meet openly? She wasn't sure she believed the answer that Taggert had given her when she'd asked him. He'd claimed it was because of the murder. That Sarah was scared either she or Michael were going to be accused of the crime. But why were they so frightened? They weren't the only ones who had a reason to hate Haydon Dapeers.

They could have been telling the truth, but Mrs. Jeffries suspected that they were hiding something else. She definitely felt that Sarah Hewett wasn't being honest. She made another mental note to have a go at Mrs. Hewett.

And what about Smythe's information? How far would James McNally go to avoid paying off his gambling debts? Before she could make any judgment about that, she had to find out how much McNally owed. No doubt Smythe would take care of that.

She smiled as she thought of Wiggins's news. It wasn't much. But then again, one never knew. Perhaps Wiggins ought to go round to the Black Horse today and find out a bit more about Ellen Hoxton. Not that Mrs. Jeffries thought there was anything to learn from that quarter. As the barmaid had just been sacked from the Black Horse, she'd probably gone to Haydon Dapeers about another position. But one never knew. It wouldn't do any harm to find out for certain. If, of course, Wiggins could find Ellen Hoxton. If she was out of work, she might be anywhere in London.

Mrs. Jeffries finished her tea. She had a lot to do today. Luty Belle and Hatchet were due round tonight after supper, Betsy was going to be snooping about seeing what she could find out about the Reverend Ballantine and Mrs. Moira Dapeers, Smythe was going to have a go at James McNally and Mrs. Goodge was expecting half a dozen of her sources through the kitchen today. She, of course, was going to tackle the inspector at breakfast and then try to find a way of having a nice, private chat with Sarah Hewett.

Inspector Witherspoon found himself back at the Gilded Lily. He was loath to admit it, but his housekeeper's gentle inquiries at breakfast this morning had got him to thinking. He'd been rather embarrassed to admit there were a number

of practical details about the murder that he hadn't attended
to.

"You wanted to see me, Inspector," Molly the barmaid
said as she bustled into the empty saloon bar.

"Yes, I've a few questions I need to ask."

"I hope it won't take long, sir. Mrs. Dapeers is insistin'
we give this place a good clean today." Molly blew a loose
strand of hair off her plump cheek. "I've ever so much to
do. Them floors in the public bar's got to be cleaned. I've
got to do the glass partitions in the saloon bar and that
ruddy Mick won't be in anymore as he's gotten himself a
position at the White Hart, so it's all fallen to me, you see."

Witherspoon smiled at her sympathetically. Poor woman,
she did look as though she worked awfully hard. Her hands
were rough and reddened from strong soaps and disinfec-
tants, her apron, though clean, was a dull gray, instead of
white, from having been washed so many times, and her
face was creased with lines of fatigue. "Do you mean, you
do all the cleaning and then were supposed to work in the
bar at night?"

"That's right. Mick refused to do anything but serve behind the counter. They had a couple of extra people hired
on the day we opened, but they was only casuals, sir. I
thought maybe Mr. Dapeers was goin' to hire someone else
t'other day, but as he went and got himself killed, I guess
nothin'll come of it. 'Corse, now that he's gone, I expect
the place will stay closed until Mrs. Haydon sells it to her
brother-in-law."

Witherspoon was genuinely sorry for the poor woman.
He certainly hoped that Tom and Joanne Dapeers would
remedy this dreadful situation when and if they bought the
place. "I promise, Molly," he said softly, "my questions
will only take a few moments."

"Well, then, what do you want to know?"

"First of all, as you know, Mr. Dapeers was murdered with a common kitchen knife. It had a brown handle and a ten-inch blade. Does that sound like it was a knife used here at the pub?" He wished he'd thought to have Barnes nip round to the Yard and get the knife from the evidence box. It would make identifying it so much easier.

Molly scrunched up her nose in concentration. "I don't rightly know. But it could have been. A brown handle you say?"

"Yes."

She thought for another moment. "I think it could have been one of ours. Hang on a tick, I'll just have a quick look in the kitchen. It's not been properly fitted out yet. Mr. Dapeers didn't want to bother with servin' meals."

"Then why did he have a kitchen in the pub?"

"It were already here when he got the place," she called over her shoulder as she disappeared down the hallway. A few moments later she was back. "There's two knifes in the cutlery drawer," she announced excitedly. "And I know we had at least two in there before."

Witherspoon felt rather foolish. He really should have investigated this question earlier. But he wasn't going to berate himself. Now he knew something very important. Very important, indeed. "Thank you, Molly, you've been most helpful. Now, could you tell me if the back door was locked on the day of the murder."

"Tighter than a bank vault," she replied quickly. "Leastways it was locked early in the afternoon. I know because we had a delivery that day from the brewery and it took me ever so long to get the door open."

"Are you absolutely certain you locked the door when the deliveryman left?"

"I didn't lock the door. Mick did."

"So as far as you know, the door could have been left unlocked?"

She shrugged. "I suppose it could, but it's not likely. Mr. Dapeers was always onto us about keeping the back door locked—" She stopped and frowned. " 'Corse, Mick might have forgot. We was busy that afternoon and there was lots of comin' and goin' through the back. Deliveries and such."

Witherspoon sighed silently. Drat. He'd so been hoping that the door had definitely been locked. If the wretched thing had been left unlocked, then anyone could have popped in and murdered Dapeers. Why hadn't he thought to investigate this matter immediately? Again, he caught himself. He really must have a bit more faith in his abilities. Obviously, his policeman's instincts hadn't considered these two matters of immediate importance. All things would come in their own good time.

"Is there anything else?" Molly asked impatiently. "I really must get crackin'. Mrs. Dapeers will be along any minute now and I've got to get them floors polished."

"Mrs. Dapeers is coming here?"

"That's right." Molly edged toward the door. "Reckon she'll be wantin' to check the place is clean as a whistle before she closes it up."

Betsy stared at the small, rather dilapidated redbrick building on the corner of Conner Street. A set of three stone stairs led up to a door with peeling white paint and a cracked fanlight in the transom. She hesitated, wondering if she was at the right place. Just then the front door opened and a young man wearing a rumpled dark suit and spectacles came out.

He started in surprise. "Can I help you, miss?"

Betsy gave him her best smile. "Is this the Reverend Ballantine's Missionary Society?"

"Yes, it is." He smiled shyly. "Would you like to come inside?"

"Yes. I'd like to make a donation, please," she said boldly. She'd decided the best way to get inside the place and have a go at asking a few questions was to offer them a bit of money. Not much, mind you. Just a pound or two. Betsy wasn't by any means rich, but for the past year someone in the household at Upper Edmonton Gardens had been leaving useful and rather expensive little gifts for all of them. Because of that person—and Betsy suspected she knew good and well who it was—she could spare a quid or two in her quest for clues.

"How very kind you are, miss," the young man said.

"I don't have much, you see," she said innocently. "But I've heard about the good work your society does and I'd like to help."

"Do please come in," he invited, turning and opening the door for her. "You must meet the Reverend Ballantine. He'll be ever so grateful for your gift."

Betsy followed him inside. They walked down a short, dingy corridor and into a small room fitted out as an office cum sitting room. There was a huge rolltop desk in one corner and the far wall was fitted with shelves and filled with books. A settee and two chairs separated by a low table stood next to the empty fireplace. The carpet was threadbare, the curtains thin enough to read a newspaper through and the wallpaper stained with water spots.

"Reverend Ballantine," the young man said to a tall man standing in front of the bookshelves. "This young lady would like to make a donation."

The man turned slowly.

Betsy tried not to stare, but it was absolutely impossible.

The Reverend Ballantine was the handsomest man she'd ever laid eyes on.

His hair was blond and had a natural wave off his forehead, his cheekbones were high, his mouth beautifully shaped and his nose strong and masculine without being too big.

"That's very kind of you, my dear," the reverend replied, smiling at her out of the bluest eyes she'd ever seen.

His voice was rich, deep and as perfect as the rest of him. But she wasn't one to have her head turned by male beauty, she reminded herself sharply. Well, maybe a bit turned. But not for a moment would she forget why she was here. "I've heard about the good work you do," she began, "and I thought I'd pop round and see if I could help a bit."

"How did you hear of us?" Ballantine came forward and reached for her hand. He pulled her gently toward the settee. "Please, do come over to the settee and sit down."

Betsy noticed that the young man disappeared. She sat down on the settee. Reverend Ballantine sat down next to her.

"Thank you," she said politely, frowning as she realized he was sitting so close he was crowding her into the corner. "But I'm sure you're a busy man and I won't take up too much of your time."

"I've plenty of time, my dear." Reverend Ballantine edged closer, his knee almost brushing hers. "Please, do introduce yourself."

Betsy took a deep breath. She really didn't much like lying to clergymen, even ones that sat too close for comfort. "Amy Lumley."

"And are you from around here, Miss Lumley?" Ballantine asked.

"No. I'm from Blackpool. I'm just down visiting my

aunt. A friend of hers is a great believer in your work. She told me all about you.'' The words came out in a rush. Though she was beginning to think that handsome or not, there was something she didn't quite like about Reverend Ballantine, Betsy simply wasn't used to lying.

"That's most gratifying,'' Ballantine said. "Will you be staying in London long?''

"Oh no, I'm on a bit of a holiday,'' Betsy replied. "But I must get back to Blackpool. I've a position there as a housekeeper.''

"A housekeeper.'' He gave her that breathtaking smile again. "Goodness, we could certainly use you here. Reginald and I try to keep the place up, but with only a cleaner coming in once a week, we don't do a very good job. All of our money, you see, goes into the society.'' He waved his hand around the tatty-looking room. "Unfortunately, doing God's work can often mean living in somewhat tiresome conditions.''

She stiffened as his movement had his knee brushing against hers. Betsy tried to edge away from him, but as she was already backed into the corner, there wasn't anyplace for her to go. "I don't have much to give. Just a pound.''

"All gifts are welcome,'' he replied, shifting slightly so that his thigh was almost flush against hers. "The Lord does provide and I really shouldn't complain. We won't be here much longer.''

"Really?'' Betsy said. She eased away from him. "Why's that?''

"Because God has sent us a miracle. Why, only a few weeks ago I was praying that we might have the funds to continue our work, and lo, it happened.'' He shifted closer to her.

"A miracle,'' Betsy repeated. She was starting to panic. He didn't act like any clergyman she'd ever come across before. His thigh was definitely rubbing against her; she could feel it through her skirt and petticoat.

"A miracle." Ballantine leaned closer, his mouth inches from her lips. "Of course, it was really quite dreadful how it happened. One of our staunchest supporters, a fine lady, very charitable; her husband died. I'm afraid he wasn't as giving as his wife. But as the Lord chose to take him, the lady can now give us all the money she wants without fear of recriminations from her spouse. Rather a miracle, isn't it? And now the Lord has sent us another miracle."

"Another miracle?" Betsy repeated.

He reached over and laid his hand on Betsy's. "You."

Luty Belle Crookshank glared at her butler. "I'da been just fine if you hadn'a interferred."

"Madam," Hatchet said as he took his employer's arm and practically dragged her out of the Fighting Cock Tavern, "you were almost hit over the head with a flying beer mug." He hurried her out into the street.

From inside the Fighting Cock, the argument that had broken out only moments ago was degenerating into a full-blown brawl. Luty glanced longingly at the door her stiff-necked butler had just hustled her out of. She sighed as she heard the familiar sound of chairs being tossed about and glass breaking. "Kinda reminds me of home," she said.

"Really, madam." Hatchet pulled her toward the corner where the carriage was waiting. "I leave you alone for two minutes and then I have to rescue you from a common tavern fight." He clucked his tongue in disgust.

"Rescue me," Luty snapped, outraged at the suggestion. "I'll have you know I'm right good at takin' care of myself. And if you hadn't come back, stickin' yer nose in and draggin' me off, I'da found out what I wanted to know."

"If I hadn't come back," he retorted, opening the door

of the carriage and shoving his mistress none too gently inside, "you'd have been hurt or arrested. But I suppose gratitude is too much to expect. By the way, precisely why were you in that disreputable place?"

" 'Cause that's where the man I wanted to question went and I couldn't stand outside and shout my questions at him."

"But I thought you were going to talk to the Dapeerses' old housekeeper."

"I did," Luty explained irritably. "But she's half-senile. Her son used to work for Dapeers too, but he spends most of his time drinkin' at the Fighting Cock, so I went after him. I was doin' real good too, pouring beer down his throat like it was water so his tongue was nice and loose. Then them two idiots at the next table started in on each other about politics and things got right heated."

Hatchet banged on the roof of the carriage and the driver pulled away. Really, there were moments when he thought his mistress ought to be kept on a leash. After spending all day yesterday talking to footmen and maids about Haydon Dapeers, they'd found out absolutely nothing. A chance remark from one of his butler friends about the Dapeerses' former housekeeper had led them to this miserable neighborhood south of the Thames. Hatchet had left Luty safely ensconced in old Mrs. Rawdon's parlor and had gone out to buy some pastilles for his sore throat. When he'd returned, Luty was gone. Luckily, he'd spotted the bright yellow feathers on her hat as he'd passed the open door of the Fighting Cock. The truth was, he wasn't in the least surprised to find his employer in the midst of a brawl. It certainly wasn't the first time. "What did you find out?"

"Plenty," Luty replied. "This fellow, Rawdon's his name, told me that Haydon Dapeers was about the meanest snake this side of the English Channel. Do you know he

fired Mrs. Rawdon just because his sister-in-law, Sarah
Hewett, was movin' into the house. Said she could earn her
keep by keepin' his house. And her a young widow with a
child.''

"Rawdon told you this?"

"Nah, old Mrs. Rawdon told me. She's only partially
gone in the mind. The minute I mentioned Dapeers she
snapped right to and started talkin' faster than a traveling
showman.''

"What else did she tell you?" Hatchet asked irritably.
He'd found out a thing or two himself, but the fact that he
could gloat over it didn't mollify him one bit. His mistress,
annoying as she was, could easily have been hurt in that
horrible tavern.

Luty grinned wickedly. "Well, seems she was doin' a
bit of snoopin' the day that Sarah Hewett and her little girl
moved into his house. Actually, she was probably listenin'
at the keyhole. Old Dapeers waited until his wife had gone
out to some missionary society she belongs to, then he hustled his sister-in-law into his study.''

"Well, what did he say?"

Luty sighed. "That's the problem. Mrs. Rawdon is goin'
deaf. She couldn't hear all that good. But she did hear Dapeers tell Sarah Hewett that she'd better do what he said
or he'd tell everyone. 'Corse, she only heard that part
'cause Dapeers was screamin' at the girl.''

Hatchet sniffed. "Is that all?"

"Is that all?" Luty repeated. "Seems to me I found out
a sight more than you have.''

"I wouldn't say that, madam." Hatchet smiled maliciously. "I haven't been idle since our return from Scotland.''

"Why, you old sneak," Luty cried. "You told me yesterday you hadn't learned very much.''

"I've reassessed the information I picked up," he informed her grandly. "And in light of what you've just told me, I think it might have some bearing on this case."

"Well," she demanded. "Tell me."

"I think, madam"—he picked a piece of nonexistent lint off the sleeve of his immaculate black coat—"that I ought to wait until we arrive at Upper Edmonton Gardens. You know how I hate repeating myself."

"All right, then," Luty said tartly, "in that case, I'll wait till we're at the inspector's before I tell what else I found out today."

"Found out from who?"

"From that drunk Rawdon," she snapped. "And believe me, it'll put what little piddling things you learned to shame."

"I've never been in a place like this before," the young woman said softly. She glanced around the crowded Lyons Tea Shop and smiled as the waiter pushed a trolley loaded with cakes, pastries, buns and tea to their table. "It's ever so nice of you to do this for me. Me Mam says I oughtn't to talk to strangers, but you're all right. I can tell, you see. You're not at all like some."

Smythe felt lower than a worm. He'd done some things in his life that he wasn't proud of, but this was the first time he'd ever taken advantage of a woman's loneliness for his own purposes. His conscience niggled at him like a bit of meat caught between his teeth. "I'm right pleased to buy you tea," he said softly, and he meant it. She seemed like a nice girl. But she wasn't very pretty. Her hair was frizzy and brown, her complexion bore the marks of a long-ago bout with the pox and her teeth stuck out in front. He'd approached her because he'd seen her coming out of the McNally house. As she wasn't used to men paying attention to her, it had been almost sinful how easy it was to strike up a conversation.

"Thank you." She smiled as the waiter put their tea on the table and then left.

"What's your name?" he asked. "You never did say."

"Velma Prewitt." She blushed slightly and looked down at her lap.

Smythe felt like the worst of blackguards. Her shy smiles and blushes convinced him the poor girl was as innocent as a baby lamb. She'd no idea he had any ulterior motives. Velma was no doubt thinkin' he was really interested in her and all he was doin' was usin' her. He cleared his throat. "My name's Smythe."

She raised her gaze and smiled. "That's a lovely name. Would you like me to pour?" she asked, nodding at the teapot.

"That'd be fine."

"You're a coachman, you said?" she inquired, lifting the heavy china pot and carefully pouring the tea into the waiting cups.

"That's right," he replied. "Work for a Scotland Yard police detective."

"Then we've something in common." She laughed. "We both work for the law. My employer is a barrister. Well, young Mr. McNally is only a solicitor, but his father is a QC."

"That's interestin'." Smythe picked up his cup of tea. He hadn't a clue how to get her talking. But blimey, he didn't want to go home without learnin' a ruddy thing. "So how long have you worked in that 'ousehold?" he asked, saying the first thing that popped into his head. He knew one thing, he had to keep her chattin'. Once he got her rattlin' on a bit, he could lead the conversation around to where he wanted it to go. Namely, James McNally.

"Not long." She helped herself to an iced tea cake. "They're decent people to work for." She hesitated and gave him a timid smile. "Well, not as bad as some places I've worked."

"That's nice," he said. Bloomin' Ada, he must be losin' his touch. He weren't able to think of a ruddy thing to say. Too bad he'd gotten in the habit of buyin' information off people. That was his trouble. He had more money than he knew what to do with, and on the last few cases he'd gotten shiftless and lazy. Now he couldn't think how to bring the subject round to where it needed to be. Blast a Spaniard anyway, this wasn't the first time his money had caused him trouble. He frowned, remembering he had to try to fit in a visit to his ruddy banker today. The silly git kept pesterin' him with letters. His last one had been right nasty. Old Pike virtually threatened to come round to Upper Edmonton Gardens if Smythe didn't stop in to the bank and give them instructions about his latest investment.

"Is everything all right?" Velma asked softly.

Smythe started. "Yeah, why?"

"You were frowning."

"Sorry." He pushed his money problems to the back of his mind. He'd deal with Pike later. He had enough worries trying to get this shy, homely young woman to confide in him and glarin' at the poor girl wasn't helpin' none. He gave her a cocky grin. "I was thinkin' of something else."

"Oh good." She gave him another shy smile. "I thought perhaps something I'd done had made you angry."

"Don't be daft, I'm enjoyin' myself," he lied. "So, I guess your employer must treat you decent, then."

"Oh yes. Mind you, I work hard. But I'm a parlor maid now. I started out in the scullery, but that was ages ago and I've worked my way up."

"That's nice. You must be a real 'ard worker," Smythe

said expansively. Perhaps if he flattered her she'd relax a bit and start talkin'. "Startin' in the scullery and workin' your way up to parlor maid takes some doin'."

"I do my best. How does your police inspector treat you?" she asked.

"He's a real gent, 'e is." Smythe helped himself to a bun. "Kind. Decent. Takes good care of 'is 'ousehold."

"So you like him, then?"

"Sure I do," he replied. "Wouldn't stay there if I didn't."

"Don't think I'd like it much," she murmured, dropping her gaze to her lap as though she were frightened by her own boldness.

He stared at her curiously. " 'Ow come?"

"Well"—Velma raised her chin and stared him straight in the eye—"I guess you could say it was because I hate coppers."

CHAPTER 7

——❦——

"Thank you for coming," Mrs. Jeffries said to Sarah Hewett. As she hadn't given her much choice in the matter, she'd been relieved when she'd spotted the woman and a small child coming into the park. She smiled down at the little girl peeping from behind her mother's skirts. "I take it this is your daughter?"

"This is my Amanda." Sarah smiled and stroked the child's golden curls. Then she looked up, her smile vanishing. "I told Moira, Amanda needed to get out in the air. It's not good for her to be shut up all day in a house of mourning. That was my excuse for getting out, you see."

"Did you need an excuse to leave?" Mrs. Jeffries asked gently.

Sarah laughed harshly. "Not really, I suppose it was just habit. It was a good idea, meeting here in the park." She gently pulled the child out from behind her dress. "Amanda, say hello to Mrs. Jeffries."

Amanda stared at the housekeeper for a moment then grinned. "Hewwo," she lisped.

"Hello, Amanda."

The little girl pointed to the open space in front of the park bench where the two women stood. "Pway," she babbled. "Pway, pway."

"All right, darling," Sarah said, "but stay right here where I can see you."

Amanda skipped off a few feet and plopped down. Immediately, she began picking up twigs and tossing them into the air.

"How old is she?" Mrs. Jeffries asked.

"Two and a half," Sarah said. She sat down on the bench, her attention riveted on her child. "And she's the most precious thing in my life. I'd die if I lost her."

"Is that what Haydon Dapeers was threatening you with?" Mrs. Jeffries asked quietly. "Taking your child from you?"

Sarah turned her head and regarded Mrs. Jeffries speculatively. "The only reason I'm here at all is because Michael insisted that talking to you might be easier than talking with the police. I didn't want to come."

"Mr. Taggert is correct," Mrs. Jeffries replied, returning the young woman's direct gaze with one of her own. "Talking to me will be a lot easier for you than speaking to the police. Providing, of course, that you didn't murder Haydon Dapeers."

Sarah jerked her head around to look at her small daughter. "I didn't kill him. But I'm not sorry that someone else did. You must promise me, Mrs. Jeffries, that what I'm about to tell you will go no further."

"I can't make you that promise—"

"It has nothing to do with Haydon's death," Sarah interrupted quickly. "It's about my daughter."

Surprised, Mrs. Jeffries glanced at the little girl. She was now lying on the soft grass and kicking her feet in the air. "Your daughter?"

"Yes, but I'll not say a word unless you give me your promise."

Mrs. Jeffries hesitated. "All right, providing the information you give me isn't connected to Haydon Dapeers's death, I give you my word it will go no further."

Relieved, Sarah sagged against the back of the park bench. "Good. Michael's sure we can trust you. I hope he's not wrong. But you asked me if Haydon had threatened to take Amanda from me. The answer to that is no. He had no interest in her. All he wanted to do was to ruin her life."

Mrs. Jeffries stared at her. "How could he possibly do that? She's little more than a baby."

Sarah stared blankly into space for a moment, then her gaze focused on the child. "He could have done it easily. All it would have taken was for Haydon to tell the truth about Amanda and her entire life would have been in shreds."

Mrs. Jeffries cast a quick glance at the little girl. There was nothing odd looking about the child at all. In fact, she was exceptionally beautiful. "Your daughter appears perfectly normal to me," she murmured, wondering if the poor thing was deaf or perhaps a bit slow mentally.

"Do you know what it's like to be a foundling?" Sarah's voice dropped to a whisper. "A bastard?"

"No," Mrs. Jeffries said softly, "I don't." Anguish flashed in Sarah's eyes, her cheeks flamed pink and her mouth trembled. "But I imagine you do," she finished.

Sarah's eyes widened in surprise and then she laughed bitterly. "You're very astute, Mrs. Jeffries. I know precisely what it's like. You see, I am one."

"I'm sorry."

"Growing up was awful," Sarah continued. "The whispers behind my back, the fact that other children wouldn't play with me: it was terrible. I would do anything to make sure my child didn't suffer the same fate. You see, when my mother found herself unmarried and pregnant, she had no choice but to throw herself on the mercy of her family. They didn't quite turn her and me out on the streets, but they made both our lives a living hell.''

Mrs. Jeffries gazed at her sympathetically. She knew the woman wasn't exaggerating. Intelligent and well-spoken, Sarah Hewett was obviously from a reasonably well-off home. Judging by her accent and carriage, her family apparently had enough income to ensure she was decently educated. Coming from her background, Mrs. Jeffries had no doubt her life had been utterly miserable when she was growing up. If she'd been illegitimate and poor, that would have been different. Not better, perhaps, since living in poverty was certainly miserable enough, but different in the sense that generally the child wasn't shamed constantly by those around them. Mrs. Jeffries had observed that poor people were far more tolerant of those born on the ''wrong side of the blanket'' than other classes were. Judging from the expression of remembered humiliation and shame she'd seen on Sarah's face, the young woman had probably spent her entire childhood being blamed for something she'd had no control over. ''How awful for both of you.''

''Haydon found out''—Sarah glanced quickly around to make sure no one else was in earshot—''that Amanda wasn't fathered by my husband. He told me if I didn't behave myself, he'd make sure the entire world knew the truth. I couldn't let that happen. I wasn't going to let it happen, and then he got murdered.''

''Most conveniently.''

Sarah gave her a sharp look. ''I may have hated him, but I didn't kill him. And neither did Michael.''

"How did Dapeers find out about Amanda's parentage?" Mrs. Jeffries asked.

"Be careful, darling," Sarah called to the little girl, who was now running around in wide circles, her arms extended like wings. "Haydon was good at finding out secrets." She sighed. "It was one of his few talents. I suppose I ought to start at the beginning."

"That would be most helpful."

"Before Amanda was born, I lived with my aunt. My parents had both died and Aunt Lillian took me in when I was eighteen. She was a great friend of Moira's family. She had this huge house, you see, and when her income was reduced because the shares her husband had invested in lost value, Aunt Lillian began taking in boarders to make ends meet. Oh, she didn't advertise or anything like that, but she rented rooms to young people from good families. One of those young men was Charles Hewett, the man who became my husband." She paused and coughed delicately. "Charles fell in love with me right away. He was a good man, kind, decent. Honorable. But at the time I wasn't interested. I was in love with someone else."

"Michael Taggert?"

She nodded. "Then I got pregnant."

Mrs. Jeffries remembered the protective way Michael Taggert had hovered over Sarah yesterday at the pub, the way he'd looked at her. "And Michael wouldn't marry you?"

"I didn't tell him." She looked down at her hands. "Michael had just gotten a chance to go to Italy to study under a master painter, I couldn't take that away from him. So I said nothing. I was terrified. Charles found me crying one day in the drawing room, he asked me what was wrong and I told him. He offered to marry me to give my child a name. We eloped that night. Amanda was born eight months later. She was born long enough after the wedding to keep most of the gossip quiet and she was quite small when she was born, so both Aunt Lillian and Charles put it around that she'd come early.''

''If there wasn't any gossip and both your aunt and your husband claimed the child was early, how did Haydon Dapeers know Amanda wasn't Charles Hewett's daughter?'' Mrs. Jeffries queried.

''Unfortunately, Charles kept a diary. I meant to throw it away after he died, but I never got round to it. I don't know how Haydon found it; I kept it locked in my trunk. But he managed to get his filthy hands on it. Charles, of course, had written the truth in the diary.''

''Why did it matter to him? Did he try to blackmail you?''

''He couldn't,'' Sarah said bluntly. ''I've little money. Charles didn't leave me well-off. But it mattered to Haydon because it gave him power over me. Haydon liked to control people. He liked moving them about like they were puppets or pieces on a chessboard. He had no real interest in me or my daughter, he just wanted to keep us under his power.''

''He didn't try to pressure you into a more, shall we say intimate relationship?'' Mrs. Jeffries asked.

Sarah closed her eyes briefly and cringed. ''He tried. But I fought him off. After that, I was careful not to be alone in the house with him. Then Michael came back from Italy. Haydon was really a coward. I think he knew that if he tried to touch me again, Michael would hurt him.''

Mrs. Jeffries frowned. Something didn't make sense here. ''If Haydon was frightened of Michael Taggert, why did he hire him to do the artwork on his new pub?''

''Haydon didn't. Moira did.'' Sarah smiled faintly. ''Moira knew Michael's work from when she used to visit

Aunt Lillian. She insisted that if Haydon wanted any money from her, he had to use Michael to etch the windows and do the wood carving. Haydon was livid, but he needed the money, so he did as she asked. But Haydon had his revenge. After he hired Michael, he threw us together and then stood back and watched us suffer.''

"How?"

"Haydon knew I'd never tell Michael the truth. I couldn't tell him he had a daughter and that I loved him and I always had.''

"Why can't you tell him the truth?" Mrs. Jeffries asked. Surely there was no reason for the two young people not to be together now. Neither of them was married.

"Because Michael would insist on acknowledging Amanda," Sarah whispered miserably. "He'd want to change her name and tell the whole world she was his. I couldn't allow that. I couldn't allow my child to be branded a bastard.''

Mrs. Jeffries thought Sarah Hewett was being overly protective. Certainly, in some circles, it would be considered scandalous. But as the child's parents would be married, she would hardly be considered a bastard any longer. However, considering what Sarah herself had gone through as a child, she could understand the woman's anxiety about it, even if she didn't agree. "Is it possible that Haydon might have told Mr. Taggert the truth?"

"No," Sarah cried, "Michael doesn't know."

"Are you absolutely sure?"

Mrs. Jeffries thought about her talk with Sarah Hewett all the way back to Upper Edmonton Gardens. She didn't like to think of either Sarah or Michael as a killer, but both of them did have a motive. With Michael Taggert, it could be as simple as rage. Sarah, an overly protective mother, could

have thought murdering Dapeers was the safest way to ensure that he never breathed one word of scandal about her
child.

Furthermore, she told herself as she hurried down the
back hall and into the kitchen, there were a number of un-
answered questions surrounding both of them. But she
quickly pushed the problem of Sarah Hewett and Michael
Taggert to the back of her mind when she walked into the
kitchen.

Inspector Witherspoon, a plate of food in front of him,
was sitting at the kitchen table. "Ah, Mrs. Jeffries," he
cried happily. "I've been waiting for you. I do need to ask
your advice about something rather important."

Mrs. Jeffries smiled brightly. "Do forgive me for not
being here, sir, but I had to—"

"Take them bad biscuits back to the grocer's," Mrs.
Goodge put in quickly. "I've already told the inspector
that."

"Yes," she replied, grateful for the cook's quick thinking, "I've been to the grocer's. Excuse me, sir, but why
aren't you eating in the dining room?"

Mrs. Goodge, standing out of the inspector's line of
sight, rolled her eyes heavenward.

"Oh"—he waved his fork in the air—"I didn't want to
bother Mrs. Goodge with running up and down the steps.
As Betsy had to go to the fishmonger's and Wiggins is over
at the boot mender's, I thought I'd just have a sit-down
here."

"I see." Mrs. Jeffries glanced at the cook, once again,
grateful that Mrs. Goodge had covered for them all. "What
would you like my advice on?" she asked eagerly. Finally,
the man had come to his senses and was going to start
talking about this case. It was getting odd, investigating
without the inspector's information, a bit like poking about

in a dark room. If they weren't careful, she and the rest of the staff were going to start banging into one another.

"Well, it's rather awkward," he replied. He pushed his now empty plate to one side.

Mrs. Jeffries realized he was probably embarrassed because he hadn't confided in her earlier. "Now, now, sir," she said soothingly, taking the seat beside him and giving him her most encouraging smile, "I'm sure you'll find that if you just tell me what it is, you'll find me most sympathetic and helpful."

"Well"—he smiled hesitantly at the cook—"I'm not certain I can really explain what I need. . . ."

"Try, sir," Mrs. Jeffries encouraged. Goodness, he really was embarrassed. But there was no need. She certainly wouldn't gloat or make inappropriate remarks.

He cleared his throat and cast another quick glance at Mrs. Goodge. But she ignored him and stubbornly continued to cut up apples.

"Actually," he said, "it's a rather delicate matter."

"I'm sure it is, sir," Mrs. Jeffries said. "And I assure you, I'm most discreet." She wished he'd get on with it. For goodness' sakes, this wouldn't be the first time he'd discussed his cases with her. Perhaps it was Mrs. Goodge's presence that was inhibiting him.

"All right, then." He took a deep breath. Gracious, this was becoming far more difficult than he'd anticipated when he'd decided to seek his housekeeper's assistance. "You see, it's a bit complicated."

"Most things are complicated, sir," Mrs. Jeffries said magnanimously. "All your cases are very complex. But you always solve them, don't you?"

He stared at her blankly. "Cases? Oh no, Mrs. Jeffries, I'm afraid you don't understand. I don't want to discuss this case with you. As a matter of fact, I'm trying a new method of detecting on this one.''

Stunned, she sat bolt upright in her chair. ''You don't?''

''Oh no.'' He smiled happily. ''This case is really quite simple, Mrs. Jeffries. As a matter of fact, I'm making a few inquires, and once those are done, I expect to make an arrest quite soon. Yes, indeed, it's really a very simple matter.''

Mrs. Jeffries couldn't believe her ears. He was going to be making an arrest soon! But that was impossible. This case wasn't simple. It wasn't simple in the least. They had half a dozen suspects and all of them could easily have committed the crime. But what could she do? A knot of panic twisted her insides. The inspector was going to make a grave mistake, she just knew it. And it would probably ruin his career.

Witherspoon didn't appear to notice his housekeeper had turned pale. ''I need your advice on a far different matter,'' he said blithely. ''A most delicate matter; one could even say, a matter of the heart.''

As she didn't have a clue what he was talking about, she simply looked at him. He was heading for disaster. She knew it. She could feel it in her bones. Before you could say Bob's-your-uncle, he'd arrest the wrong person and then he'd find himself back in the records room at Scotland Yard.

''Mrs. Jeffries, I do realize this isn't a normal housekeeping duty, but I need your help most desperately.'' He blushed like a schoolboy. ''You see, Lady Cannonberry's letter to me was most . . . affectionate, shall we say. And I need a bit of help in drafting an equally affectionate reply to her.''

That evening, as soon as dinner was over, Mrs. Jeffries didn't waste one moment. The moment Luty and Hatchet arrived, she bade them sit down, poured them both a cup of tea and then plunged right in and told them about her strange encounter with Inspector Witherspoon.

The others were as surprised as she had been except for Mrs. Goodge, who'd been in the kitchen when the Inspector had made his shocking announcement.

"You mean he's close to an arrest?" Luty asked in disbelief. "But that's impossible. We ain't told him nuthin'."

" 'Ow does 'e know who the killer is when we don't?" Wiggins exclaimed.

"Was 'e 'avin' you on a bit?" Smythe asked incredulously.

"Excuse me, madam," Hatchet said politely. "But are you sure you understood the inspector correctly?"

"He were dead serious," Mrs. Goodge replied angrily, not giving Mrs. Jeffries time to open her mouth. "And if he's not careful, he'll not only ruin his career with the Yard, but he'll muck up our lives good and proper too. Who does he think he is? Makin' an arrest, indeed. He can't possibly know who the killer is."

Mrs. Jeffries felt somewhat as the rest of them did; however, she did feel she owed Inspector Witherspoon's detecting abilities some show of respect. "Well, perhaps we're all being a bit too hasty. Perhaps he knows something about this crime that we don't."

Smythe shook his head. " 'E can't. I've spent two days talkin' to people about that killin' and there couldn't be anything 'e knows that we ain't found out. Just take this McNally person; I found out today that 'e was at the Gilded Lily the night of the murder. Maybe 'e weren't inside the pub, but 'e were seen 'angin' about the back door."

"Does the inspector know about McNally?" Hatchet asked.

" 'E couldn't," Smythe replied. "Accordin' to what

Velma told me, 'e 'asn't been round to ask any questions.''

"So he doesn't even know McNally is a suspect," Mrs. Jeffries said thoughtfully. "Yet he feels he's on the verge of an arrest. We can't let it happen. Arresting the wrong person at this point will ruin his career."

"How can we stop it?" Mrs. Goodge cried. "He's not even talking to you? We don't know what he knows, and even worse, he doesn't know what we know! Why I even found out a few bits myself. Mind you, it wasn't easy, seein' as how the victim was only a publican."

Mrs. Jeffries decided that wasting any more time lamenting Inspector Witherspoon's odd behavior would be foolish on their parts. "What were you able to find out, Mrs. Goodge?" she asked the cook.

"Well, it's not very nice, it isn't, but I had a chat with Rupert Simmons, he's my cousin's second husband's nephew and he works at the house right up the road from where the Dapeerses live. Rupert told me that he heard from the upstairs maid at the Dapeers house that Mrs. Dapeers has been carryin' on with some preacher. And what's more, she didn't much care if the whole neighborhood knew about it. She's completely taken leave of her senses over this man. Of course, this Reverend Ballantine is supposed to be as handsome as sin, not that he sounds like much of a man of the cloth to me."

Betsy, who vividly remembered the awkward moments she'd spent that very afternoon at the Reverend Ballantine's Missionary Society, felt a blush creeping up her cheeks and dropped her gaze to her lap. "He *is* handsome."

Smythe gave her a sharp look. " 'Ow do you know that?"

"Yes," Mrs. Goodge asked tartly, giving the maid an irritated frown, "how did you find out what he looks like?"

Betsy glanced up and saw that everyone was staring at

her. "Because I saw him, that's how. And Mrs. Dapeers is giving him pots of money now that her husband's dead and can't nag her anymore. The fact is that Reverend Ballantine told me himself that his society was coming into a lot of money. Called it a miracle, he did."

"Did he actually say he was getting money from Moira Dapeers?" Mrs. Jeffries asked.

"He didn't use her name, but from what he told me, I could tell it had to be her."

"He told ya?" Smythe exclaimed. "And when did you meet 'im?"

Betsy glared right back. Just because she and Smythe occasionally "walked out" together didn't mean he could boss her about. "This afternoon. I went round to the missionary society—"

"And this Reverend Ballantine just up and answered all your questions?" Smythe interrupted. He didn't know that he wanted Betsy out and about and talking to strange men. Especially ones that was handsome as sin.

"Of course not," she snapped. "I didn't let on anything about the murder. It just came up in conversation, that's all."

Mrs. Jeffries could tell by the expression on the coachman's face that he was bedeviled by a touch of the green-eyed monster, so she quickly said to the maid, "Were you able to find out anything else?"

"Not really. But Reverend Ballantine did seem to think that he'd had a miracle come his way. I'm certain he was talking about Dapeers's murder. I think Mrs. Dapeers is in love with him, and what's more, he knows it and is usin' it to get what he wants from her." Betsy quickly told them the rest of her tale and why she'd come to the conclusion that Moira Dapeers wasn't precisely a grieving widow. The only part she left out was the embarrassing details, such as how she'd finally had to give the good reverend a sharp kick in the knee and then bolted like a hare to get out of that house!

"You've done well, Betsy." Mrs. Jeffries gave her an approving smile. "It seems quite clear that Moira Dapeers did have a motive for killing her husband, if, indeed, she is in love with this man Ballantine."

"So did Sarah Hewett," Luty put in. "I found out that Haydon Dapeers was tryin' to make her his mistress. He was holdin' something over her head, threatening to tell everyone some dreadful secret of hers if she didn't coop-erate with him."

"And how did you find out that bit of gossip?" Hatchet asked irritably. As it was precisely the gossip he'd heard, he was most annoyed with his employer for stealing his thunder.

Luty smiled smugly. "From Rawdon; you know, he was talkin' real good before that brawl broke out."

"Brawl?" Mrs. Goodge exclaimed. "What brawl?"

Before Luty could explain, Hatchet said, "I had to rescue Madam from a rather unfortunate incident at a pub this afternoon."

"Rescue me!" Luty snorted indignantly. "I'll have you know I was doin' just fine. I can still hold my own, you know. Just 'cause I'm old don't mean I can't skedaddle outta the way when a few fists start flying."

"Oh dear," Mrs. Jeffries murmured. One of her greatest fears of having Luty and Hatchet involved in the inspector's cases was that the elderly woman would get hurt. "You could have been hurt, Luty."

"Fiddlesticks! This ain't the first time I've seen a fight—"

"Speakin' of fights," Wiggins interrupted excitedly. "I talked to a couple of people that were in front of the Gilded

Lily the night of the murder; they was actually watching the fight.''

''Did any of these people remember who they saw standing outside the pub?'' Mrs. Jeffries asked. There was really no point in badgering Luty; she was far too stubborn to listen to any of them. ''I mean, could they alibi any of our suspects?''

''What do you mean?'' Mrs. Goodge asked.

''She means,'' Smythe said smoothly, ''that if any of the suspects was actually seen watching the fight, then they couldn't 'ave been skulkin' down to the taproom and stickin' a knife in Dapeers.''

''Precisely.''

''Well''—Wiggins bit his lip—''the men from Bestal's was seen outside. I know that 'cause the bloke I was talkin' to told me he wondered what they was doin' at the Gilded Lily.''

''Selling beer,'' Mrs. Goodge said. ''That's why they was there, to sell beer.''

''But that's not true,'' Wiggins insisted. ''Harry told me 'e knew for a fact that the Gilded Lily was gettin' their supply from Midlands Ale. That's why he noticed the men from Bestal's; he'd seen them in the Black Horse and he wondered why they'd gone to the Lily.''

''Maybe the gentlemen from Bestal's was tryin' to change Dapeers's mind about using Midlands,'' Betsy suggested.

As Mrs. Jeffries didn't think who Dapeers bought his beer from had anything to do with the murder, she decided to move things along. ''The important thing is that we've now eliminated the gentlemen from the brewery. Does anyone else have anything to add?''

''Only that McNally was really desperate,'' Smythe said quietly. He winced inwardly as he remembered Velma

Prewitt. "Accordin' to what I found out, McNally's father was goin' to boot 'im out of the 'ouse if 'e found out about the gamblin'. Seems he'd paid his son's debts one time too often in the past. Velma told me—"

"Velma?" Betsy asked archly. "How come you never seem to talk to cabbies and porters anymore when we're on a case? Now it's always women you're chattin' up."

Smythe, delighted to get a bit of his own back, gave the maid a wicked grin. "Can I 'elp it if the ladies love talkin' to me."

"Hmmph," Betsy snorted delicately. "And I'll bet you love talkin' to them too."

Drat, thought Mrs. Jeffries, now Betsy had a touch of the green-eyed monster too. Really, she wished these two would make up their minds about each other. Normally their bantering didn't bother her, but on this case, she was finding it definitely annoying. "I think I'd better go next," she said firmly. "Unless, of course, you have any more to add, Smythe."

He shook his head.

Hatchet said, "I found out that Haydon Dapeers was in financial straits. According to my sources"—he gave Luty a superior smile—"Dapeers had overextended himself opening the Gilded Lily. His suppliers were threatening him. Furthermore, I heard that the gambling debt that James McNally owed wasn't a paltry amount. It was two thousand pounds. Two thousand pounds Dapeers desperately needed if he was going to make his new pub successful."

"And we know that McNally was there that night," Mrs. Jeffries said. "If only we knew if the back door was locked or not."

"McNally could 'ave used the side entrance, the one off Bonham Road to get in," Smythe suggested.

"And he could have used the back door, or the front

door, or climbed in an open **window**," Mrs. Jeffries said in disgust. "The point is, we're guessing. We're starting to jump to conclusions and we really must stop. What we need are facts."

But facts were difficult to find in this case, she thought irritably. They had far too many suspects, far too many motives and far too little information from the inspector. "We'll just have to keep at it," she said firmly. "And we'd better do it as quickly as possible. I have a terrible feeling that if we don't come up with some decent evidence soon, the inspector is going to make the worst mistake of his life."

Witherspoon grimaced as he took a quick taste of the pale ale. Gracious, the Black Horse looked like a nice pub, but the beer was dreadful. It had no taste at all.

"Stuff tastes awful," Barnes hissed in his ear. "It's a wonder they have any trade." He glanced around the crowded public bar.

"Well, until the Gilded Lily opened up, there wasn't much competition around here. The nearest pub is a quarter of a mile up the road."

"No wonder Tom and Joanne Dapeers was so upset about Haydon Dapeers opening a pub just up the street from 'em," Barnes mumbled. "I'd be worried too."

"You wanted to speak to me, Inspector?" Joanne Dapeers said as she came into the bar.

"Good day, Mrs. Dapeers." Inspector Witherspoon smiled politely. "I realize you're busy, but I've a few more questions to ask."

Joanne shrugged prettily. "All right, though I don't know what else there is to say. I told you everything I know."

"Could you tell me precisely where you were standing

when the fight out on the street broke out.''

''Where I was standing? Hmm . . . let's see now,'' she replied thoughtfully. ''I was standing by the window, Inspector. Yes, that's it. Most everyone else ran outside when it started, but I had a full glass of ale and I didn't want to spill it, so I went over and stood by the table and watched out the window.''

''And do you remember if anyone else stayed inside?'' Witherspoon asked.

Her brows drew together as she concentrated. Finally, she said, ''I'm sorry, Inspector, I was watching the brawl, I wasn't looking around me to see who was where or what was going on inside the pub. But I do recall one thing.''

''And what's that?''

''Well, when everyone came back inside and I went to find Haydon, I remember being relieved to see that Michael Taggert hadn't come back inside with Sarah. She was standing at the bar on her own. I was afraid Michael and Haydon would have another ruckus.''

Witherspoon stared at her. ''Are you absolutely certain about this?''

''Oh, absolutely,'' she replied, picking up a clean hand towel from underneath the counter and flinging it open. ''Like I said, they'd already had trouble that evening, so I was right relieved to see that he'd taken himself off. Come to think of it, I don't recall seeing Taggert in the bar before the fight started, either.''

''But I thought you weren't paying attention,'' Barnes said.

She shrugged. ''I wasn't. But now that you mention it, I do recall having a quick look around to see if he was chattin' up Sarah, and he'd disappeared. This was right after Haydon went to the taproom.''

"Mrs. Dapeers, what made you go looking for your brother-in-law?"

"You mean when I found Haydon's body?"

"Yes."

"Well, I've already told the police all this. It's not something I want to think about again."

"I'm sure it was an awful experience for you, Mrs. Dapeers," Witherspoon said sympathetically. "But please, do go over it once again." He really didn't like asking a lady to recount what must have been a dreadful experience, but after thinking about it, he'd decided that he must. Mrs. Dapeers may have seen or heard something important that night without even realizing it.

"Well, there's not much to tell, really," she replied. "People were drifting back in because the constable had broken up the fight outside. I realized it was getting late and that we'd better get back, so I went down the hall to say good night to Haydon. I'd noticed he'd not come out of the taproom. When I got there, he was lying on the floor with a knife in his back. I screamed and people came running in."

"Did you see anyone?"

Joanne shook her head. "No one. Just Haydon lying there."

Tom Dapeers came out of the back and went behind the bar. He put his arm protectively around his wife. "It's not very nice for her to have to talk about it again," he complained.

"I'm sorry, but it was necessary. Thank you for your help, Mrs. Dapeers."

"If you've finished, Inspector, the wife and I have work to do."

"I am finished. I'm sorry to have interrupted your busy day."

Tom nodded and he and Joanne disappeared back into the hall.

"Odd her rememberin' Taggert's movements," Barnes muttered. "And no one else's."

"Yes, but she did have a specific reason for keeping an eye on Taggert," Witherspoon said slowly. "He and Haydon Dapeers had already had one heated exchange. She seems a strong-minded sort of woman, but perhaps even she didn't want to watch another brawl. Especially after that one out in the street."

The inspector absently picked up his tankard and took a sip, grimacing as he swallowed. His head whirled with bits and pieces of information, none of which made sense or pointed him in the direction of the killer. Perhaps he really ought to talk about this case to his housekeeper; perhaps listening to his inner voice wasn't such a good idea after all. . . .

"Give us a tankard, Tom," a man shouted from the other end of the bar. "And while you're at it, see if you can come up with some decent entertainment. We ain't 'ad anything 'appen round 'ere since that fight the other night."

Witherspoon's eyes widened as he turned his head and stared at the burly figure at the far end of the bar. Gracious, he thought, why hadn't he thought of it before? Putting down his drink, he turned and hurriedly went over to the heavyset man in the flat cap and porter's coat. Barnes, taken by surprise, caught up with him a moment later.

"Excuse me, sir," the inspector said politely, "but did you actually see the fight in front of the Gilded Lily?"

The man grinned. "It were a good one too. 'Ad me a front-row seat. Best bit of brawlin' I've seen in a long time."

"And where were you standing while you were watching the brawl?" Witherspoon asked.

"I were standin' across the road from the pub." Then his face creased in a suspicious frown. "What's it to you? Who the bloomin' 'ell are ya, anyway? And why you askin'?"

"I'm Inspector Witherspoon from Scotland Yard and I think, sir, you may be able to help us with our inquiries."

Fifteen minutes later the inspector had finished questioning Tim Magee. He had more information, but for the life of him, he couldn't quite decide what it all meant.

But he now had a few hard facts. The inspector took comfort in that. Even if nothing quite made sense yet, he was beginning to get the glimmer of an idea about this murder. He nodded to himself. Yes, it might be a very simple case after all. Very simple, indeed.

Constable Barnes tapped him lightly on the shoulder. "Here comes Constable Griffith, sir," he said, pointing to the uniformed officer pushing his way through the crowd.

"Good day, sir, Constable Barnes." Griffith nodded respectfully. His cheeks were flushed and he was out of breath, as though he'd been running. "I've been sent round to collect you, sir," he said to the inspector. He glanced quickly around the pub and saw people openly staring at them. "You'd best come with me, sir." He dropped his voice to a whisper. "There's been another stabbing. Only this time it's a woman."

CHAPTER 8

Smythe reluctantly pulled another bill out of his pocket and slid it across the table. "You're a bloomin' robber, that's what you are, Blimpey. But you done good, so I expect I oughtn't to complain."

He was disgusted with himself for having to buy information again, but in this case, there really wasn't anything else he could do. They were running out of time. According to Mrs. Jeffries, the inspector could be getting ready to make an arrest. And considerin' the man didn't have a clue about this case, it would lead to disaster.

"Ta, Smythe, you're a gentleman." Blimpey grinned and pocketed the cash. "Must say I was kinda surprised gettin' that message from you today. Didn't think you'd want to keep doin' business with me after the other day. Sorry about that, but like I said, I've got me reputation to think about."

Smythe shrugged. In truth, he'd been right narked at Blimpey, but seein' as the man could find things out quicker than a bank manager could grab your money, he hadn't had much choice. "You're sure you've got yer facts right about Michael Taggert?"

" 'Corse I'm sure." Blimpey laughed, but as he was taking a drink at the time, it came out as a wet snort through his nose. Smythe ducked to avoid being sprayed by the worst-tastin' beer in all of London.

"Sorry," Blimpey apologized, and wiped the spray off the tabletop with his shirtsleeve. "Michael Taggert hated Dapeers's guts, and he didn't take that job with Dapeers 'cause he needed the lolly. Taggert come into an inheritance two months ago. He's got more money than you or I, mate, and that's the truth of it."

"Then why work for a man you 'ated?" he mused. Yet he thought he knew the answer to that question already. Especially if Taggert were really in love with Sarah Hewett. Smythe too had more money than he'd ever spend, and he continued to work for the inspector. But he didn't have any choice. If he said anything, if the others at Upper Edmonton Gardens knew about it, things would change. They'd be different; he'd have to leave and that would be more than he could bear. Leaving would mean he wouldn't be out and about solvin' murders, there'd be no more familylike evenins' with the others, and most of all, he wouldn't be able to see Betsy every day. After hearing what Mrs. Jeffries had told them yesterday, he thought he understood why Taggert took the job at the Gilded Lily. It kept him connected to Sarah.

"Don't know, mate," Blimpey replied airily. "If I 'ad Taggert's fortune, I wouldn't be 'angin' about bein' a slave for someone like Dapeers. I'd be livin' it up in fine hotels and drinkin' French wine—"

"From the way you're downin' this swill," Smythe interrupted, nodding at the tankard of beer in front of Blimpey, "you wouldn't know French wine if it come up and bit you on the arse."

Blimpey laughed. "You got me there, mate, but it's the thought that counts. If I had plenty of lolly, I'd call no man master. Seems to me this Taggert's off his 'ead, but what can you expect, 'e's an artist. They're an odd lot. Even stranger, Taggert's kept real quiet about inheriting his money. It took me a good bit of snoopin' about to find it out."

Smythe wondered if Sarah Hewett knew. He had a feeling she didn't. She was in love with Taggert and at the same time she wanted to protect her child from scandal. Seemed to Smythe the best way to do it would have been to marry the child's father. But she hadn't. Why? The more he heard, the more convinced he was that the only one of the two lovers who had a real motive to kill Haydon Dapeers was Sarah, not Michael Taggert. Unless'n Taggert was so enraged by the victim's attempts to seduce his woman that he killed Dapeers in a fit of anger. But the killing hadn't been done in a fit of rage—it was too neat and tidy for that. "I wonder if Sarah Hewett ever come down to the Gilded Lily while it was bein' fitted out?" he murmured. If he was right in his thinkin', then Taggert taking the job with Dapeers would make sense.

"Is she Dapeers's sister-in-law?"

"Yeah, 'ow did you know?"

Blimpey shrugged. "I pick up lots of things, you know that." He took another swig of ale and belched softly. "I don't usually give out for free," he said slowly. "But bein' as yer such a reliable customer, I'll toss you this one on the 'ouse. I already know the answer to that question. Sarah Hewett was at the Gilded Lily a lot when it was bein' kitted out. She come with Moira Dapeers. Seems Haydon insisted the ladies come round every day or so and have tea with him in the afternoon. Used to drive the workmen barmy. And the ladies didn't like it either. The Hewett woman was always complainin' about 'aving to leave her brat with the maid and Mrs. Dapeers was on about 'ow comin' to the bloomin' pub interrupted her afternoon.''

Smythe nodded, satisfied that he had his answer. Rich or not, Michael Taggert had worked for Dapeers because it was the only way he could see Sarah Hewett. It made perfect sense to him. If the only way Smythe could see Betsy every day was to hang about workin' for someone, he'd do it. "Why did Dapeers want them there, do ya think?"

Blimpey, who was quite an astute judge of human nature, shrugged. "To torment 'em, probably. Me sources tell me that Taggert were crazy about Sarah Hewett, made sure he was at the pub workin' every afternoon when she come round. Dapeers acted like a right old bastard every chance he got, yellin' at Taggert, tellin' 'im this was wrong an' that needed to be fixed. Sounds to me like Dapeers made the women come in just so's 'e'd 'ave a chance to act like God Almighty and belittle the lot of 'em. And me sources said it was obvious there was no love lost between Dapeers and his wife either. Molly said the woman barely spoke to her 'usband.''

"So they all 'ated 'im.''

"And any of 'em coulda killed 'im,'' Blimpey agreed. "But I'd put my money on one of the women. Taggert's rich enough now that if 'e wanted to murder Dapeers, 'e could hire it done.''

"James McNally had a motive too,'' Smythe argued. Maybe he was gettin' sentimental, but he didn't like to think of Michael Taggert as a murderer. Or Sarah either.

"True.'' Blimpey drained his tankard. "But 'e's not got the guts. McNally just about pissed 'imself when I told 'im Dapeers wanted his lolly. Can't see a man like that 'avin'

the nerve to sneak up on a bloke and stick a knife in 'is
back.''

James McNally was a nervous, rabbity-looking fellow with
a long, bony face, pale skin and a growing bald spot on the
back of his head. Betsy stared at the bald spot as she followed him down Meeker Street. She had no idea why she
was following McNally, except that she couldn't think of
anything else to do and she, like the others in the household, felt she had to do something. The inspector might be
getting ready to ruin all their lives.

Betsy couldn't stand the thought that her dear inspector
might find himself back in the records room and, even
worse, that she and the household wouldn't have any more
murders to solve.

McNally turned a corner and disappeared down a passageway between two brick buildings. Betsy hesitated at
the entrance. She'd been following him for what seemed
hours, and without her even realizing it, she was now on
the ruddy docks. What was a respected solicitor doing
down here? Betsy had to know. She was sure he was up to
no good. But this area of London wasn't very safe. Once
she was off the street, she might be fair game for any ruf-
fian that happened to be hanging about.

She narrowed her eyes as she saw McNally was almost
through the passage. Blast a Spaniard, she thought, I've got
to do something. But the footpath between the buildings
was dark and smelled awful. To be honest, she was a bit
scared. Then she thought of never working on a case again,
of spending the rest of her life changing linens and dusting
furniture. Betsy bolted down the passageway.

Despite the summer heat, it was cool inside. She hurried,
trying hard to walk softly as she saw her prey turn a corner
and disappear from her sight. Betsy picked up her skirts

and began to run. She couldn't lose him now, not when things were starting to get interesting. She flew out the end and onto an empty wharf overlooking the river. Suddenly she was grabbed around the waist and whirled around. Betsy tried to scream just as James McNally's hand covered her mouth.

"The victim's name is Ellen Hoxton," the uniformed constable said to Witherspoon. "Been in the water a few days; you can tell by the bloat. Lucky for us, her skirt caught on that piling; otherwise she'd have been carried off by the current."

Witherspoon hated looking at bodies. Thank goodness he'd eaten a light breakfast this morning. He didn't quite trust his stomach. He'd seen victims who'd been in the water before, and they weren't a very pretty sight. But duty was duty. He knelt by the body and steeled himself to look at the dead woman. Her skin was blue-tinged and the fish had been at her. Witherspoon swallowed convulsively and glanced around the deserted dock. There was a heap of rubbish on the far side, some of the pilings were rotting, and several of the planks were missing from the deck. The place looked deserted. "Who found her?"

"I did," the constable replied. "I was chasin' a pickpocket out here and spotted her hair floating out from beneath the wharf. Of course the pickpocket got away when I stopped to investigate. When I fished her out, I knew it was murder. You can see she was stabbed right through the back."

Witherspoon took a deep breath and gently turned the body. He grimaced as he saw the wound in her back.

"It took me a few minutes to pull her free of the piling," the constable continued. "That's how come her skirt's torn so badly. When I saw she'd been knifed, I knew it was murder.''

"Indeed it is, Constable," Witherspoon murmured. He shook his head sadly, appalled that this poor woman's life had been so cruelly taken from her. "Has the Yard been notified?"

"Yes, sir, they should be here any moment. I expect they'll bring a police surgeon with them."

Witherspoon nodded. "How did you know the victim's name?"

The constable, a gray-haired grizzly veteran of well past fifty, grinned. "Oh, I've known Ellen Hoxton for years. I've arrested her more times than I can count. She's a prostitute when she can't get work as a barmaid."

"I see."

"And I know she got sacked from the Black Horse, because one of her friends was lookin' for her and asked me if I'd seen her in the past couple of days or so," the constable continued. "Thought it odd that I hadn't, sir."

"Why?"

"Because this is Ellen's part of London, sir. No matter how often she gets sacked, she won't leave the area. Considerin' that she were employed at the Black Horse, and bein' as I knew that was connected with that stabbin' at the Gilded Lily, I sent Constable Griffith to find you as soon as I realized she'd been stabbed. I expect that's what killed her, sir. The stabbin', not the water."

"Ah, I see." Witherspoon couldn't bear to look at the poor soul another minute; he certainly couldn't tell by looking at her exactly what had caused her death. He'd leave that to the police surgeon. Not that it really mattered. Drowned or stabbed, someone had murdered her. She hadn't poked a knife in her back and jumped in the Thames on her own. He eased himself away from the dead woman and rose to his feet.

"Do you think this killin' is connected to Haydon Dapeers's murder?" Barnes asked softly. He knelt by the body, turned her over and stared at the spot on her back where the knife had gone in.

Witherspoon averted his eyes. He couldn't think why his constable wanted to examine the corpse, but he had far too much respect for Barnes to try to stop him. "I really don't like to make assumptions," he began slowly.

"But she's been stabbed in the same spot that Dapeers was," Barnes persisted. He jabbed his finger at the blackened round slash. "I don't think that's a coincidence."

Witherspoon forced himself to take a quick look and then fastened his eyes on a boat going up the river. "I don't think it's a coincidence, either," he agreed. An idea began to form in his mind. A simple yet bold idea that might bring this case to a conclusion far faster than he'd imagined.

"Constable," he said to the other policeman, "who else knows you've found this body?"

The gray-haired policeman looked surprised by the question. "Well, Constable Griffith and the Yard, of course. And the police surgeon's been notified and is on his way too. Otherwise I've told no one."

Witherspoon nodded. "Good." This poor woman had had her life taken. It filled him with sadness and despair. But if he was right, if he was really the policeman everyone seemed to think he was, he'd have her killer behind bars very soon. Very soon, indeed. "Have any of the locals been back here to see what's going on?"

"No, this whole end of the docks is deserted," the constable replied. "These buildings and the wharves are scheduled to be torn down next month and rebuilt. The East India Company just bought it."

"Excellent." Witherspoon hoped his policeman's instinct wasn't leading him astray. "Please try and make sure that no one, especially the press, knows exactly where her body was found."

Barnes gently rolled the late Ellen Hoxton onto her back. He got to his feet, shaking his head. "But what difference does it make if people know where she was found? Whoever killed her probably thinks she's halfway to Gravesend by now."

"That's precisely my point, Constable," Witherspoon said briskly. "And we want the killer to go right on thinking that."

James McNally dropped his hand from Betsy's mouth and leapt back. "Oh dear, dear," he wailed in a high-pitched voice. "Why are you following me? What do you want? Please don't scream. Did my father put you up to this?"

Stunned, Betsy stared at him. "Your father?"

"It would be just like him to hire a woman to spy on me," McNally said shrilly. "It wouldn't be the first time. Are you another of those typewriter girls?" He took a step closer to her. "He tried to foist one on me before. The minx showed up bold as brass at my office last week. She was carrying that silly little machine and she told me she'd been hired to do my correspondence. But I took care of her; I wasn't going to have her clattering away on that thing, watching my every move, seeing who came and went in my office and then running and tattling to my father. I poured treacle on the wretched thing."

"You poured treacle on a typewriter girl?" Betsy repeated. She couldn't believe her ears! James McNally was mad. Absolutely, stark raving mad. And she was alone here on a deserted dock with him.

"Not on the girl, on her stupid typewriter," he explained

belligerently. "She took herself right off, she did. Ran screaming down the hall and out into the street. She wasn't there to take care of my correspondence."

"How do you know?" Betsy thought perhaps it would be best to keep him talking. At least until someone else came along or she could think of a way to get out of here.

"Because I don't have any correspondence," he said, his eyes gleaming triumphantly. "I haven't had a case in six months. My father's always complaining about that too. It's not my fault I've no clients. It's his. If he'd only leave me alone, I'm sure I could do nicely." He angled toward her. "He hired you, didn't he?"

"No, of course not." Betsy drew back and cast a quick glance around the area. The dock was still empty. There weren't even any boats out on the river. Not that she could swim. "I don't even know who you are."

He glared at her suspiciously. "Then why were you following me? Don't try and deny it. You've been walking behind me for the last twenty minutes."

"I wasn't following you," she insisted. "I was just takin' a walk and minding my own business when you grabbed me." She shot a quick look toward the end of the passageway. No help there.

"In this neighborhood?" He laughed. But the sound was harsh and ugly and made her stomach churn in fear. "I'm not stupid, you know. There's nothing here but a deserted dock. No one in their right mind goes walking in this area, even in broad daylight."

"You did." Betsy edged back a bit. If she had to, she'd make a run for the passageway. He might not catch her before she made it out to the street.

"I've business here," he snapped. "How much is he paying you?"

It didn't take too much thinking to know what he was

on about. "He's not payin' me nothin'," she yelled, hoping that by screaming at the man she'd attract some attention. She was getting tired of this and a little angry too. "Now leave off botherin' me and I'll be on my way."

She started to turn and he grabbed her arm. "You're not going anywhere until you admit he's paying you to spy on me."

"Let me go."

"Not until you tell me."

Betsy saw red. It would be a cold day in the pits of Hades before she'd put up with being handled like this. Instinctively, she made a fist of her right hand, using a method she'd been taught by some pretty tough ladies when she was a girl living in the East End. Before McNally realized what she was doing, she drew her right arm all the way back, shot it forward and smacked him right on the jaw.

"Ow . . ." He dropped her arm and leapt backward. He stumbled and fell, landing hard on his backside. "That hurt."

Betsy turned and started to run. She'd almost made it to the passageway when she realized he wasn't coming after her. She threw a quick look over her shoulder and then stopped dead.

James McNally was sitting on the dock, crying his eyes out.

"Are you absolutely certain?" Witherspoon asked. He and Constable Barnes were standing on the door stoop of a run-down lodging house near the East India Docks.

Molly, the barmaid from the Gilded Lily, shook her head. " 'Corse I'm sure. I saw her with me own eyes. I even told Mick about it. Not that the silly sod was payin' attention; he never paid attention when I said something."

"But Mick told us she left a note for Mr. Dapeers,"

Witherspoon persisted. He needed to get this right. He needed to make himself perfectly clear so that Molly understood exactly what he was asking.

Molly waved her hands impatiently. "I give Mr. Dapeers the note she left. But she come back later that afternoon."

"But Mick didn't mention that."

"Mick was too busy jawin' with the workman out in the back to notice. But she waltzed in big as you please and went right into the saloon bar with Mr. Dapeers. They talked for a good ten minutes and then she left." Molly looked pointedly at the street. "I've got to be goin', Inspector. I've got to take the rest of them linens from the Lily over to the laundry. Then I've got to get to work."

Witherspoon and Barnes both stepped out of her way as she pushed past them and started down the short path to the street. "You have a new position?" he asked politely.

Molly nodded and continued moving steadily toward the road. "At the White Hart over on Cory Place," she yelled. "It's not much of a pub, but the pay is decent. Better than what Dapeers was payin' me anyway."

"You didn't happen to overhear what they were talking about, did you?" Witherspoon scrambled after the woman. He didn't want to order her to stay put long enough to finish answering his questions. He knew how difficult employment was to come by for women of her age.

Molly stopped, turned and glared at him, offended by his question. "I don't eavesdrop on people."

"I didn't mean to imply you did," he said quickly. "I do apologize. But occasionally, one does overhear things. Why, it happens to me all the time."

She gazed at him suspiciously for a moment and then her expression cleared. "All right, I guess you're only tryin' to do yer job. I didn't hear what they was talkin' about, I was busy gettin' ready for the openin'. But I did

see Mr. Dapeers give her a fiver.'' She started toward the
street again.

"A fiver?'' Witherspoon rushed after her. "You mean
he gave her five pounds?''

She turned onto the road. "That's what a fiver is.''

"And you didn't think it important to tell us this before?''

She shrugged and started to cross the road. "I thought
he was just buyin' himself a bit o' fun, if you know what
I mean. She were known to do that every now and again.''
Molly laughed at her own wit. "And he did it all the time.
Gossip had it that he'd even tried to tumble his sister-in-
law.''

"Ruddy men, they don't listen to a word you say,'' Molly
grumbled. "I'm not even sure that police inspector knows
how to listen properly. But you're not like them, are ya,
lad?''

Wiggins smiled at the woman and heaved the heavy
wicker basket he'd just taken from her to his other hip.
"Well,'' he replied doubtfully, "I do the best I can. 'Ow
far is it to the laundry?''

"Not far.'' Molly pointed up toward the end of Bonham
Road. "It's just round the corner and then a bit. It's right
nice of ya to carry that for me. Bloomin' 'eavy, it is.''

"Don't like to see a lady such as yerself carryin' such a
load,'' he said gallantly. He'd hung around the neighborhood of the Gilded Lily all morning. When he'd spotted
Molly coming out the back door carrying a large basket,
he'd leapt at the chance to do his good deed for the day.
"What was you sayin' about the coppers?''

"Oh them.'' She waved her hands in dismissal. "They
come around askin' more questions today. It's not

like I 'adn't talked to 'em before, you know. Not my fault that no one ever listens.''

"I guess they was askin' about the murder." Wiggins slowed his steps. The basket was heavy, but he didn't want to arrive at the laundry before he found *something* out.

" 'Corse they was askin' about the murder," Molly grumbled. "Don't know why they're tryin' so hard to find the killer. Seems to me the guilty one is right under their nose. Not that I blame 'er, mind you. If my old man had brought 'ome what Haydon Dapeers did, I'd probably shoved a knife in his back too.''

"You think Mrs. Dapeers is the murderer?" Wiggins asked incredulously.

" 'Corse I do." Molly snorted in disgust. "My daughter works as a housemaid for Dapeers. She only started a month ago and she was goin' to try and find something else. But then he up and got himself murdered, so Agatha decided to stay on. She likes Mrs. Dapeers. Agatha's heard plenty in that house. Not that the police have bothered talking to her, oh no, I guess they don't think a servant's got ears. But Agatha told me plenty.''

Wiggins decided trying to worm information out of this woman was a waste of time. He could tell by the eager gleam in her eyes that she was dying to tell everything she knew. "What'd she say?"

"Well, I'm not one to be repeatin' gossip," Molly said with relish. "But Agatha overheard the most awful row a few days before Mr. Dapeers was murdered.''

"What was it about?"

Molly gazed at him speculatively. "Well, I don't think I ought to say, it's not very nice to talk about. Especially to one so young.''

"I'm older than I look." He shifted the heavy basket to

his other side. "Besides, it wouldn't be fair to stop now. I'll die of curiosity."

"I know what you mean, lad. I hate it when people do that. Well, as I was sayin', last week Agatha was cleaning out the closet in the bedroom next to Mrs. Dapeers's room. All of a sudden she heard Mrs. Dapeers screamin' at Mr. Dapeers that he was a depraved animal. Well, it frightened Agatha no end, it did. But she was like you, curious. So she leaned her ear against the wall and you'll never guess what she heard."

"What?"

"Mrs. Dapeers had found out that Mr. Dapeers had caught the shanker!" Molly shook her head, her expression disgusted. "If my old man brought somethin' like that home, I'd do 'im in, I would. I expect that's exactly what Mrs. Dapeers did."

Wiggins wasn't sure if he knew what a "shanker" was. But he didn't really want to ask. He decided he'd wait till tonight and ask Smythe. He'd know. And he wouldn't laugh at him for askin', either.

"I hope you all have had better luck than we have," Luty said glumly. She dropped down into an empty chair and stared at the circle of morose faces around the table. "From the looks of it, your luck has been about as bad as ours."

"I take it you didn't find out anything," Mrs. Jeffries stated.

"Not a dag-gone thing," Luty grimaced. "And I spent all day talking to people. No one seen anything, no one knows anything and no one heard anything."

"I told you it was a waste of time buying those street arabs sweets," Hatchet said dryly. "They only told you they'd been hanging about the Gilded Lily on the day of the murder because they overheard you questioning that cabbie.''

''I know that, Hatchet.'' Luty glared at her butler. ''But them young'uns never get sweets. I didn't hurt us none to buy 'em some. I saw you slippin' that little boy some money when you thought I wasn't lookin', so don't be jawin' at me none.''

Hatchet blushed. ''Well, the lad did look awfully thin.''

''Did anyone learn anything today?'' Mrs. Jeffries asked. She hoped someone had something to report. She'd insisted everyone return for tea in the hopes that one of them would find out something the rest of them could use.

Betsy cleared her throat. ''Well, I did find out something,'' she said slowly. She glanced at Smythe. She had to tread carefully here; she had to use just the right words to explain what had happened this afternoon. Not that McNally had really been mad, but if she didn't tell it just so, it would sound that way. In truth, once she'd got McNally to stop crying and talked with him a bit, she'd actually felt sorry for the poor fellow. But if they knew the details about her encounter, if they knew she'd been stupid enough to follow a suspect down a dark passageway and onto a deserted dock, she'd be shut up in this house polishing silver till her hair turned as white as Luty's.

''Good.'' Mrs. Jeffries smiled eagerly. ''I'm glad one of us has had some success.''

''I think we can take McNally off our list of suspects.'' Betsy smiled blandly and reached for the cream pitcher.

Everyone waited for her to continue. Betsy poured the cream in her tea and concentrated on stirring it with her spoon.

''Well, go on,'' Smythe urged. ''Tell us the rest of it.''

Betsy couldn't stare at her teacup for the rest of the afternoon, so she looked up. ''There isn't anything else.''

"Whaddaya mean, there isn't anything else?" Smythe eyed her suspiciously. There was something she weren't tellin' and that was a fact.

"Betsy," Mrs. Jeffries said quickly, "surely you have a reason for telling us McNally shouldn't be a suspect?"

"Of course I do," Betsy agreed. She swallowed nervously and looked around the table. Everyone was staring at her. Mrs. Jeffries looked concerned, Luty and Hatchet gazed at her like she'd been out in the sun too long, Mrs. Goodge was glaring at her as if she hadn't wiped her feet before coming into the kitchen and Smythe frowned fierce enough to strip paint off the walls.

"But it's a bit difficult," she continued. "You'll just have to take my word for it, he couldn't of done it." After talking to McNally, she'd come to the conclusion that the man was too timid to squash a bug, let alone stick a knife in someone's back.

"You did something dangerous, didn't you?" Smythe said softly.

Startled, Betsy jerked in surprise.

His frown, if possible, grew fiercer. "I knew it." If Betsy didn't know him so well, she'd have been afraid. "I knew you'd been out and about doin' somethin' that coulda got you hurt or even killed! I can always tell, you get all quiet and sneaky like."

"I do not," Betsy cried. "It's just that there's no need to be tellin' everyone all the details. McNally's such a nervous old thing he could no more shove a knife in someone's back than he could walk on the Thames."

"Aha, so you admit you've confronted McNally," Smythe yelled.

Mrs. Jeffries decided to intervene. Smythe was overly protective of all the household, but he was ridiculously protective of Betsy. This wasn't the first time they'd come to words about the issue and it wouldn't be the last. But right now this case was such a puzzle she didn't need an outbreak of war between the two of them. "Smythe, please. Calm yourself. I'm sure Betsy knew precisely what she was doing today. Let's not discuss this matter right now. We're already muddled enough about this case; if Betsy is sure one of our suspects can be eliminated, then I suggest we take her word for it."

Smythe looked as though he wanted to argue the point, but he contented himself with giving Betsy one last frown. "All right," he said grudgingly, "I'll put it aside. For now."

"I don't know that eliminating McNally from our list is goin' to help matters none," Luty said bluntly. "Truth is, I'm as confused as a drunken miner on Saturday night. I can't make heads nor tails of this murder and I don't think any of the rest of you can either."

For once, Hatchet didn't argue. "I agree, madam. So far, we've had a man murdered who was hated by his wife, his family, his employees and everyone else who knew him. Everyone had a motive, we have no witnesses, no physical evidence and the inspector isn't talking. I'm afraid I don't have a good feeling about this one. We may not be able to solve it."

Mrs. Jeffries was hard-pressed to disagree with him. She felt the same way. But they mustn't give up. They had to keep trying. "Let's not get discouraged," she said brightly. "I think we're doing quite well. Has anyone else learned anything today?"

"Don't look at me," Mrs. Goodge mumbled. "None of my sources could come up with anything."

"I did," Wiggins said. He wished he'd had time to have a quick word with Smythe, but he'd got home so late he hadn't had a chance.

"Excellent." Mrs. Jeffries nodded for him to continue.

Wiggins took a deep breath. "Mrs. Dapeers knew that her husband had got a nasty disease. She found out last week and screamed her head off."

"Disease?" Mrs. Goodge asked irritably. "What disease?"

"The shanker," Wiggins mumbled in a low voice. He was pretty sure he knew what it was, and he didn't think it was the sort of thing one discussed in front of the ladies.

"The what?" Luty frowned. "I didn't quite catch that."

"Speak up, Wiggins." Betsy leaned toward him. "I couldn't hear you."

"Say it again," the cook demanded.

"Did you say he had the canker?" Hatchet asked. "Do you mean canker sores? Goodness, they're quite painful, but I can't think why they should cause such distress that someone would scream about them. They're only mouth ulcers."

Smythe looked down at the tabletop. He was trying not to grin. He'd heard Wiggins quite clearly.

"I said he caught the shanker," Wiggins muttered again, raising his voice a fraction. Blimey, from the way Smythe was grinnin', he was dead sure that this disease was what he thought it was. Blast. Now he'd have to say it out loud.

"The what?" Mrs. Goodge demanded. "The shank-hill?"

"Wiggins is trying to tell us that Moira Dapeers had obviously found out her husband was infected with syphilis," Mrs. Jeffries said calmly.

CHAPTER 9

Mrs. Jeffries had done some thinking. She still wasn't certain of very much, but she did know that what she'd learned from the others this afternoon convinced her that this case was far too complex to leave to the inspector. She was determined to feed him some clues and information, whether he wanted it or not.

Consequently, she had his sherry poured and waiting by his favorite chair when he came in that evening.

"I've taken the liberty of fixing you a sherry," she announced as she took his hat from him. "You've been working so very hard on this case, I thought you might need a few moments to relax before dinner."

"That's most kind of you, Mrs. Jeffries," Witherspoon replied. "But won't Mrs. Goodge have supper cooked?"

"It's been so warm today that Mrs. Goodge thought you'd prefer a cold meal, sir." She started down the hall. "It'll keep until you've had a few moments to yourself."

He followed her into the drawing room, sat down and

picked up the glass. The liquid sloshed over the tips of his fingers. "I say, this is a rather full glass you've given me." He laughed. "Are you trying to get me drunk?"

She was trying to loosen his tongue, but she could hardly admit it. "Oh dear, how foolish of me. I must not have been paying attention when I poured it. Sorry about that, sir. So tell me, how was your day?"

Witherspoon took a sip from the overly full glass, taking care not to spill. "Oh, things are progressing nicely. By the way, did you post my letter to Lady Cannonberry?"

"Yes, sir," she replied quickly. She didn't want him to get started about that again. "Wiggins posted it this morning."

"Good, then she ought to get it tomorrow." He frowned suddenly. "You don't think I was too affectionate in my reply to her, do you? I shouldn't like her to think I'm being overly bold."

Mrs. Jeffries forced herself to smile. "You were perfectly correct in your letter, sir. Right on the mark. Now, sir, did you question more—"

"But I wasn't too formal, was I?" he interrupted. "I shouldn't like her to think I'm stuffy. Lady Cannonberry might be the widow of a lord, but you know, she's quite progressive in her thinking. Why, actually, she's a bit more than just progressive. Just between you and me, Mrs. Jeffries, I think she'd like to see some rather radical changes in our whole system. Not that we've discussed it overly much, mind you. But she does occasionally say things which I find quite extraordinary. Quite extraordinary, indeed. Do you know, she told me she thought that women ought to be able to vote and she was positively incensed at all the public funds that were spent celebrating Her Majesty's jubilee year."

"I'm sure she was, sir," Mrs. Jeffries replied. She knew

all about Lady Cannonberry's radical opinions, and for the most part she agreed with them. But she didn't wish to discuss it right now. She racked her brain, trying to come up with a conversational gambit that would get the inspector talking about this murder. "There were a number of people who felt the funds raised for the jubilee would be better spent elsewhere. Perhaps those people are right, sir."

"Do you really think so?" Witherspoon took another sip.

"Yes, sir, I do," she said firmly. "Just take this dreadful murder you're investigating. It seems to me that if we had a society that paid a bit more attention to the poor and the unfortunate, we probably wouldn't have desperate people running about killing other people."

Witherspoon waved his hand in the air. "I'm afraid I don't agree with you. Though I must admit that your comment does have merit in some cases, I've seen a number of crimes where the culprit was more to be pitied than imprisoned, but I'm afraid you're way off the mark about the murder of Mr. Dapeers."

Now they were getting somewhere. Mrs. Jeffries smiled brightly, pleased that her trick had worked. "How so, sir? I mean, it seems to me the victim might have been murdered because he walked in on someone trying to rob the pub. That person might not have meant to commit murder at all. He could have been a simple robber. Someone who might have been starving or looking for a few shillings to buy medicine for one of his children. It seems to me, sir, that if our society actually provided a bit more for people like that, they wouldn't be driven to commit crimes."

"This wasn't a murder committed by someone desperate for a few pennies to buy a loaf of bread," the inspector said quickly. "Haydon Dapeers was murdered by someone who knew him, someone who had a pressing reason to get him out of the way."

"So you know who the killer is?" she persisted.

"Well, not exactly," he replied. "But I've a good idea. A very good idea, indeed."

"Really, sir? Oh, do tell me!" she cried enthusiastically. "You know what an admirer of your methods I am. Please don't leave me in suspense. I shan't sleep a wink all night if you do." She was laying it on thicker than clotted cream, but she didn't care. At this point she'd try anything.

He smiled widely. Perhaps he should tell her what he had in mind. The plan was really quite sound. Quite reasonable. It might be just the thing to put it into words. Sound it out, so to speak. Besides, it was really too selfish of him to keep the poor woman in the dark. He knew how much his housekeeper admired him. "If everything goes as I plan," he began eagerly, "by tomorrow night, the killer will be safely under lock and key."

Mrs. Jeffries gazed at him incredulously. Had he lost his mind? Making an arrest at this stage would be fatal to the inspector's career. Absolutely fatal. There was too much he didn't know, too many suspects he hadn't even considered and too many motives for Witherspoon to have sorted it out and come up with a plan. Any plan he came up with at this stage would land the inspector back in the records room faster than you could blink your eye. She had to do something. "How very clever of you, sir. Do tell me more."

Witherspoon smiled proudly. By the expression on Mrs. Jeffries's face, he could tell she was quite stunned by his brilliance. "I've a few more details to take care of tomorrow," he continued, "but—" He was interrupted as Fred came bounding into the room.

Wagging his tail furiously, the dog leapt at the inspector, his forepaws landing on Witherspoon's knees. Fred immediately butted his head against the inspector's arm. It was the dog's favorite trick, one that guaranteed him a walk in the park.

"I'm quite pleased to see you too, Fred." Witherspoon patted the animal's head. "Do you want to go for a walk? Yes, of course you do, old fellow. We've not been walkies in quite a while."

Though Mrs. Jeffries was fond of Fred, she shot him a fierce glare. "But what about your dinner, sir?" she said as the inspector put his sherry down and got to his feet. "Aren't you hungry?"

"Oh, as you said, it's a cold supper. Come on, boy, let's go get your lead." He started for the door. "Dinner will keep."

"I want you to stick to him like a piece of flypaper today," Mrs. Jeffries told Smythe. They were all seated around the dining table in the kitchen, eating their breakfast. Mrs. Jeffries had made one last stab at getting the inspector to talk last night, but she hadn't been successful. Right after he'd finished his dinner, he'd announced he was dead tired and gone right to bed.

The housekeeper had told the others what little she'd learned of the inspector's plan, and they were agreed they had to find a way to stop him from making the worst mistake of his career.

The coachman shoved his empty plate to one side. "And 'ow exactly am I to do that?" he asked.

"You've got to think of some way, Smythe," Betsy said earnestly. "Mrs. Jeffries said he was getting ready to make an arrest. If he ends up back in the records room, the rest of us'll spend our lives polishing silver and scrubbing floors. There won't be any dashing about looking for clues and following suspects." She broke off as the coachman shot her a quick frown. She and Smythe had already had a rather heated discussion about the matter of following suspects.

"You'd better come up with something quick," the cook added. "The inspector's almost finished his breakfast."

"Bloomin' Ada, what do you want me to do? I can't just trail after the man all day, he'll see me."

"Let's think," Mrs. Jeffries said. But she'd thought about it half the night and hadn't come up with one logical reason for Smythe to go along with Inspector Witherspoon. "Perhaps you could just follow him at a distance."

Smythe shook his head dismissively. "I don't think that'll work. I'd 'ave to stay too far behind, otherwise the inspector or Barnes would notice. Barnes is a right smart copper; not much gets past 'im."

"We've got to come up with something," the cook cried passionately. "I refuse to give up investigatin' murders just because Inspector Witherspoon's got a bee up his bonnet about listening to his 'inner voice.' I won't give it up, do you hear? This is important. For the first time in my life I'm doin' something that matters. Really matters. We all are and we're not goin' to get the wind knocked out of us just because the man's got some idea he can solve this one on his own."

"What do you suggest?" the coachman snapped, goaded into anger because he agreed with everything Mrs. Goodge said and was just as scared as she was that it was all coming to an end. "I can 'ardly make myself invisible."

"There's no call to be rude, Smythe," Betsy said, raising her voice.

"All this arguing isn't solving our problem," Mrs. Jeffries began.

"I've got an idea," Wiggins said softly.

Everyone turned and stared at the lad.

"*You've* got an idea?" Smythe said incredulously.

The footman blushed. Maybe his idea wasn't so good after all. Maybe he should have kept his mouth shut.

"Don't be sarcastic," Mrs. Jeffries said. "Let's hear what Wiggins has to say."

"Seems to me it's right simple," Wiggins said nervously. "Seems to me that all Smythe 'as to do is tell the inspector that Bow and Arrow is lookin' peaked because they ain't been out in the fresh air for a long time. Smythe could offer to drive the inspector to wherever he needs to go today." He waited for the others to tell him his plan was silly.

But no one said a word for a moment. Finally, Smythe said, "Out of the mouths of babes." He grinned broadly. "You've done it, lad, you've come up with the solution. The inspector's daft about them 'orses. 'E loves 'em."

"It *is* a good idea," Mrs. Jeffries said. She smiled at Wiggins and then glanced at the clock. "How fast can you get the carriage here?"

Smythe was already getting to his feet. "Fast enough. I'll pop upstairs and ask the inspector if it's all right."

"Lay it on thick, Smythe," Mrs. Jeffries said as he started for the backstairs. "You must stay with him today. You're our only hope."

"What do you want the rest of us to do?" Betsy asked as soon as Smythe was gone.

Mrs. Jeffries had thought about that too. She wasn't sure where the inspector was going with this case, but after listening to him last night, she'd come up with one possible scenario. "This morning, I want you to get out and find out as much as you can. I'll leave where you go and what you do up to you. At this point finding out anything might be helpful."

"In other words, you're as muddled as we are about this

case, so it doesn't really matter what we do," Betsy said glumly.

"Correct." The housekeeper smiled sadly. For all the thinking she'd done, she really hadn't any idea who the killer was or why the victim had been killed. She didn't think the inspector had any idea either. But she didn't think that would stop him from making an arrest. However, she refused to acknowledge defeat. There was one thing she could do to mitigate what she was sure was going to be a disaster. If they were lucky, she might buy them enough time to solve this case. But right now her first task was to keep the inspector from making a complete fool of himself and losing the precious reputation they'd worked so hard to give him. Tomorrow they could go back to work on catching Haydon Dapeers's killer; today they had to avert a disaster.

"But just because we haven't solved this particular puzzle doesn't mean we won't. Get out there and find out what you can. As I always say, any information is useful. You never know what little bit of gossip you'll pick up that will be the missing piece we need to put it all together." She got to her feet. "I would like all of you back here this afternoon. Wiggins, could you please pop around to Luty's and tell her and Hatchet to be here as well. We don't know what's going to happen tonight and we ought to be here in case we have to do something drastic."

"What are you going to be doin' this mornin'?" Mrs. Goodge asked.

"I'm going to go and see Sarah Hewett," Mrs. Jeffries said. "If my idea works, I'll be bringing her back with me this afternoon. Betsy, I'd like you to take a note around to Michael Taggert's house. Make sure he reads it. If he shows up here before I get back, don't let him leave."

Smythe was just coming out of the dining room when

Mrs. Jeffries got upstairs. " 'E **went for the idea,**" he whispered, jerking his thumb toward the closed door. "I'll be back in a bit with the carriage. But 'e said something funny, though. 'E said 'e was plannin' on askin' me to 'elp 'im out with something tonight. This plan of 'is, I reckon."

"Excellent, Smythe," Mrs. Jeffries replied. "And whatever he asks you to do, do it."

"You don't need to tell me that, Mrs. J."

"I'm sorry. Of course I don't." She started for the front door. "In any case, stay close to him. We're all depending on you. You may be the only thing standing between Inspector Witherspoon and the records room."

Mrs. Jeffries reached for the brass knocker on the late Haydon Dapeers's front door. She hesitated for a moment, wondering if she was doing the right thing. But there was no other answer. She'd thought and thought about every aspect of this case. If she were wrong, she might be interfering in a private matter which could be disastrous to the people involved. But if she was right, she might be saving Sarah Hewett untold misery and grief. She knocked on the door.

A maid answered. "Can I help you, ma'am?" she inquired politely.

"I'd like to speak with Mrs. Hewett," she replied.

The maid showed her inside and then led her down the hall to the drawing room. "If you'll wait here, ma'am, I'll see if Mrs. Hewett is receiving."

A few moments later Sarah rushed into the room. "What are you doing here?"

"I need to talk to you," Mrs. Jeffries said firmly. "Is there someplace where we can speak in private?" She didn't want Moira Dapeers suddenly popping in on them.

"We can talk here." Sarah frowned in confusion. She

gestured at the settee. "Moira's gone to the missionary society."

"Good. Then we won't be interrupted." Mrs. Jeffries sat down.

Sarah sank down next to her. "I really wish you hadn't come here," she began.

Mrs. Jeffries interrupted. "I'm sure you don't," she said bluntly. "But believe it or not, I'm here to help you."

"Help me?" Sarah repeated. "But I don't need help."

"Did you tell the inspector everything you told me about your movements on the night of the murder? Did you tell him you'd gone back into the pub *before* the brawl on the street was over?"

"Well, yes," Sarah said defensively. "I wasn't going to lie to him."

"And you also told him that while you were inside the room was empty and you saw no one?" Mrs. Jeffries pressed.

"I told him that I was there for a few moments on my own and that I hadn't seen anyone go down the hall toward the taproom," Sarah said gravely. "But I also told him that several other people began to drift in while I was still at the bar."

"Did any of those people see you standing at the bar?"

Sarah shrugged helplessly. "I don't know. I wasn't paying attention."

"Do you know any of those people who came in?"

"They were all strangers. That's what I told the inspector. But what's that got to do with anything?" she cried shrilly, her voice rising in panic. "I tell you I was there. I was standing by the bar. Why are you here? Why are you trying to scare me?"

"You need to listen to me very carefully. I'm not here

to cause you grief or stir up trouble, but it's imperative that you do precisely as I say.''

Sarah's eyes were as wide as saucers. ''Why? Why should I do anything you tell me?''

''Because if you don't, you might be arrested for the murder of Haydon Dapeers.''

Mrs. Jeffries was still wondering if she was doing the right thing when she arrived home at Upper Edmonton Gardens. She took her hat off and hurried down the stairs to the kitchen. Luty Belle, Hatchet, Betsy, Wiggins and Mrs. Goodge were sitting around the kitchen table, their expressions glum.

''Hello, everyone,'' Mrs. Jeffries said brightly, determined to lift all of their spirits.

There was a general murmur of greeting, but it was singularly lacking in enthusiasm. Mrs. Jeffries hadn't seen so many long faces at one table since Mrs. Edwina Livingston-Graves, the inspector's dreadful cousin, had visited them last year.

''Sarah Hewett will be here about one o'clock.'' She took her usual seat and smiled at Betsy. ''Did you get the message to Michael Taggert?'' she asked.

Betsy nodded. ''Yes, I saw his landlady give it to him myself.''

''What's this all about, Hepzibah?'' Luty asked. ''We've been sittin' here like a bunch of sinners waitin' for the angel Gabriel to blow his trumpet for judgment day. Would you mind tellin' us just what in tarnation is goin' on?''

''Yes, madam,'' Hatchet added. ''Not that we object to making ourselves available to the cause of justice, but young Wiggins here''—he smiled at the footman—''was not forthcoming with any details. He merely told us you needed us here 'in case the inspector makes a right old muddle of the murder.' ''

Mrs. Jeffries glanced at Mrs. Goodge. ''Didn't you tell them the inspector is planning on making an arrest?'' she asked.

''They ain't told us nothin','' Luty said, not giving the cook time to answer.

''We weren't sure exactly how to explain things,'' Mrs. Goodge said quickly. ''So we thought we'd wait until you got back.''

''I see.'' She quickly brought them up to date on the latest developments. ''So you see, we've got Smythe carting him about in the carriage today, hoping, of course, that he might be able to do something if the need arises.''

''All right,'' Luty said thoughtfully, ''I understand all that. But why is Sarah Hewett and this Taggert fellow coming here this afternoon?''

''Because I'm afraid the inspector is going to arrest Sarah Hewett,'' she said. ''She's the only one of all the suspects that the inspector could think is the killer.''

Luty looked confused. ''How do you figure that?''

''Because she's the only one who has admitted being in the public bar while the murder was committed instead of being outside watching the street brawl.''

''Excuse me, madam,'' Hatchet said politely. He glanced at Luty. ''But do you really think Inspector Witherspoon would arrest someone on that kind of evidence?''

Mrs. Jeffries didn't think so, but she was hard-pressed to come up with any alternative suspects. ''I don't know. But if the possibility exists, I think it's important that Sarah tell Michael Taggert the truth about her daughter before it happens.''

For a moment no one said a word. Then Betsy said, ''I can see how you might think the inspector's going to arrest her: she's admitted to him she was alone in the pub, probably at the same time the murder was bein' committed. But how is her telling Michael Taggert the truth about him bein' Amanda's father going to help any?''

"It won't stop the inspector from arresting her, but at least it will give her the chance to ensure that Amanda is taken care of properly while she's awaiting trial or in prison," Mrs. Jeffries explained.

"Wouldn't Moira Dapeers take care of the child?" Hatchet asked.

"Not necessarily, not when Sarah's motive—the fact that the child was fathered by someone other than Moira's brother—comes out. If the case goes to trial, it will come out.''

"We don't even know that the inspector knows anything about that," Luty pointed out.

"We found out, didn't we?" Mrs. Jeffries shot back. She was feeling most put upon. She could tell by their expressions that they all thought she was grasping at straws. The awful thing was, they were right. She'd no idea what the inspector knew, she'd no idea what he was planning on doing or who he was going to arrest tonight. "For all we know, Haydon Dapeers could have told someone else about Sarah's daughter. That person could have mentioned it to the inspector.''

"Well," Mrs. Goodge said slowly, "I think you've done the right thing." She got up. "I think I'll fix us all a spot of something to eat. No use sitting around here being miserable. That may happen soon enough if the inspector ruins his career tonight.''

Witherspoon stuck his head out of the coach and yelled at his coachman. "I say, Smythe, this is rather the long way around. It'll take us ages to get to the Yard at this rate. The traffic's dreadful.''

''I'll see what I can do,'' Smythe called. He sighed as the inspector ducked back inside the coach. Of course the ruddy traffic was bad; that's why he'd picked comin' down this bloomin' street in the first place. Cor blimey, he thought, he didn't have any idea what to do now. There was no help for it. He'd dawdled all he could, taken the carriage down every crowded street he could find in the hopes of delaying things a bit, but he was at his wits' end. He had to drive the inspector to Scotland Yard. Witherspoon was going ahead with his plan, whatever in blazes it was. But Smythe knew one thing: the inspector's plan involved more than a few coppers. That's why they was goin' to the Yard. Blast a Spaniard anyway, the inspector was fixin' to make a ruddy mess of things tonight and he was goin' to have half of the Metropolitan Police Force there to watch it.

Smythe grimaced at he turned the coach onto Charing Cross. They'd been all over London today. They'd been to the Black Horse, the Gilded Lily, Michael Taggert's lodging house and the Dapeers home. At each stop, Witherspoon and Constable Barnes had gotten out, popped inside, stayed a few minutes and then popped back out again. Smythe had no idea what they were up to, but he didn't like it much.

But he could dawdle no longer; Scotland Yard was just ahead. He slowed the horses and pulled the brake. Witherspoon and Barnes both climbed out as soon as they'd stopped. Smythe stared at them glumly. ''Do you want me to wait here for you, sir? Or should I pull the carriage to one of the side streets?''

''You can leave it here, Smythe.'' Witherspoon beamed

at him. "I'll send a uniformed man out to keep an eye on it. I need you to come with me."

Smythe tied the reins off and jumped down. "You need me, sir?"

"Well, I might. I've got to run my idea by the chief inspector first, though. But tell me, Smythe, are you any good at playacting?"

Promptly at one o'clock, Sarah and Amanda Hewett arrived at Upper Edmonton Gardens. As instructed, after a brief introduction, the rest of the household, including Luty and Hatchet, took Amanda and went outside to the communal gardens.

"I almost didn't come, Mrs. Jeffries," Sarah admitted. "But then Inspector Witherspoon came around and told Moira and me we had to be at the Gilded Lily tonight."

"Did he give you a reason why?"

Sarah closed her eyes briefly. "He said he had an important piece of evidence he had to ask us about," she replied softly. "And that we had to be there in order to see it."

"What time do you have to be there?"

"Eight o'clock." Her voice dropped to a whisper and tears welled up in her eyes. "But I think he's going to arrest me. He asked me again about being in the public bar. He wanted to know if I'd remembered the names of anyone else who was inside then."

"And of course you hadn't," Mrs. Jeffries said sympathetically. "Do you feel up to this?"

Sarah nodded mutely. She grasped the back of the chair for support and took several long, deep breaths. "What if he doesn't come?"

"He'll come," Mrs. Jeffries promised. "As a matter of fact, I expect I'd better go upstairs in a moment, to let him in. Pour yourself a cup of tea. I'll send him down as soon as he gets here.''

Sarah sat down but didn't make a move toward the waiting china teacup sitting next to the pot of freshly brewed tea. She stared blankly into space. ''I don't know if I can do it.''

''Would you rather he find out from someone else?''

''But what if he hates me? What if he despises me for not telling him straightaway?'' She swiped at an escaping tear. ''I don't think I could stand that.''

Mrs. Jeffries tried to think of something sympathetic or comforting. She was having second thoughts about everything. Maybe she had jumped the gun, so to speak. Maybe Witherspoon had no intention of arresting Sarah. Maybe she'd interfered in a very private matter and the end result would be disastrous. Maybe, she thought, I'd better get upstairs. Sarah could use a few moments alone.

She was halfway up the stairs when she heard the heavy bang of the brass knocker. Mrs. Jeffries hurried her steps, threw open the door and smiled at Michael Taggert. ''Good afternoon,'' she said pleasantly. ''Please come inside.''

''Good day,'' Taggert replied as he stepped through and into the hall. ''Your note said it was urgent.''

''It's about Mrs. Hewett,'' Mrs. Jeffries explained.

''Sarah? Sarah's here?''

''She's downstairs in the kitchen waiting for you.'' Mrs. Jeffries pointed to the backstairs. ''Right down there.''

Without another word he rushed toward the staircase and hurried down it, his footsteps echoing so fast on the stairs that Mrs. Jeffries hoped he didn't fall flat on his face. Explaining to Inspector Witherspoon how one of his suspects ended up at the bottom of the kitchen stairs with a broken leg wasn't something she really wanted to do.

She debated for a moment, wondering if she should try

to eavesdrop on the two young people. This was, after all, a murder investigation. Even though she didn't think either of them was the killer, she wasn't sure. On the other hand, their conversation was personal and private. "Oh bother," she murmured as she headed for the front door. "I refuse to eavesdrop on such a private conversation. If either of them is the killer, I'll eat my hat."

"Sarah, what are you doing here?" Michael asked. He stood at the door of the kitchen. "I've been out of my mind with worry ever since I got that strange note from Mrs. Jeffries. She said you were in trouble?"

"I might very well be in trouble," Sarah replied. "But before we talk about that, I've got something I must tell you." She got up from her chair but didn't move. She simply stood there. "It's something I should have told you a long time ago, but I didn't have the courage."

Concerned, he went to stand beside her. "I don't understand any of this. But don't worry, my love. Whatever kind of trouble you've got, we'll see it through. I won't let anyone hurt you."

"Michael, please sit down and listen to what I have to say. There may not be much time." She sat back down and waited until he took the seat next to her. "Before I say anything else, I want you to know how much I love you."

Michael grabbed her hand. "And I love you. Now tell me, what kind of trouble?"

She shook her head vehemently. "Not yet. First there's something you've got to know. Something you must understand. I have to know she'll be safe if the worst happens. I have to know she'll be taken care of by someone who loves her."

Alarmed, Michael grabbed her by the shoulders. "Darling, what are you talking about? What do you mean 'if the worst happens'?''

Sarah swallowed the lump in her throat and then looked him dead in the eyes. "Amanda is your daughter, Michael. Not Charles Hewett's."

"How long they gonna be?" Wiggins complained. "I'm gettin' hungry again."

"Stop your moaning." Mrs. Goodge smiled as she watched Hatchet duck behind a tree, hiding from the laughing Amanda. "Them two aren't talking about the weather, you know."

"Do you think it'll be all right?" Betsy asked anxiously. She glanced at the back door of Upper Edmonton Gardens. "They've been in there a long time."

"I hope so," Mrs. Jeffries replied.

"Caught ya." Luty, holding Amanda's hand, tagged Hatchet as he pretended to run from the little girl. Amanda giggled uproariously.

"Well, I wish they'd 'urry," Wiggins said, frowning at the back door. But his frown vanished suddenly. "Blimey, 'ere they come."

Everyone, except the child, turned and saw Michael and Sarah coming out the back door.

He took Sarah's hand and together they crossed the lawn toward the others.

Amanda, seeing her mother, came running out from behind the tree she'd been hiding behind. She stopped suddenly and stared at the tall man holding her mother's hand.

Luty, Hatchet, Wiggins and Betsy had all come to stand in a group next to Mrs. Jeffries.

Michael Taggert knelt down and looked at the beautiful

little girl watching him. Tears filled his eyes.

"I think," the housekeeper said softly, "that we'd better go inside. Mr. Taggert may like some privacy when he meets his daughter."

CHAPTER 10

⟫⟩∘⟨⟪

"I know that neither of them is the murderer," Mrs. Goodge announced. She sniffed and swiped quickly at her eyes, wiping back the sentimental tears that threatened to roll down her cheeks.

" 'Corse neither of 'em is the killer," Luty agreed. "It's got to be one of the others. Why, did you see the way that man looked at his little girl? I tell ya, he had tears in his eyes, he was so happy. A feller like that ain't capable of murder and you only have to look at Sarah to know she couldn't do it."

"But the inspector thinks it might be Sarah," Betsy said worriedly. "What if he arrests her tonight and that poor little baby loses her mama?"

"It'd be a crime, that's what it would be," Wiggins agreed. "Separatin' a mama and her child ought to be against the law."

Mrs. Jeffries glanced toward the back hall and hoped she hadn't made the mistake of her life. They were all sitting at the table in the kitchen, waiting for Sarah, Amanda and Michael to come inside. Everyone had been deeply moved by what they'd just witnessed. Now they were all convinced that Amanda Hewett was a darling little angel, Sarah Hewett was a saint and Michael Taggert a knight in shining armor.

Mrs. Jeffries was at this point fairly certain that at least Sarah was innocent. Getting the woman to come here had been a kind of a test. She'd reasoned that though Sarah was adamant about keeping her daughter's parentage a secret— in fact, that was really her only possible motive for wanting Haydon Dapeers dead—she'd come here anyway. She'd stood in front of a group of strangers and introduced her child to its father. If Sarah had been truly unbalanced enough to murder to keep the world from knowing Amanda wasn't Charles Hewett's daughter, she would never have done what she did today. Sarah wasn't guilty. Mrs. Jeffries was sure of that. But what about Michael Taggert? He'd had motive enough. He'd watched the woman he loved stay a virtual prisoner in the Dapeers house. Maybe he'd finally had enough.

They heard the back door open. Everyone turned, their attention on the back hall. Sarah Hewett, followed by Michael carrying Amanda, came into the kitchen.

"Do come in and sit down," Mrs. Jeffries said. "We've some tea made. I expect you could both do with a cup."

Sarah smiled shyly and sat down next to Mrs. Goodge. Michael Taggert took the chair next to Wiggins. He settled Amanda on his lap and then said to Mrs. Jeffries, "Tea would be nice, thank you."

"Your little one's almost asleep." Mrs. Goodge nodded at the child, who was dozing against her father's chest. "Should I take her? There's a daybed in my room; it's right down the hall. You can hear her if she wakes up and gets frightened. She can have a bit of lay-down while you two have your tea.''

''Uh . . .'' Michael, uncertain in his newfound role as parent, looked at Sarah.

''That would be lovely, thank you. It's way past time for her nap.'' Sarah got up, plucked the sleeping child off his lap and followed the cook out of the kitchen.

''I don't know how to thank you for what you've done,'' Michael said to Mrs. Jeffries. ''Sarah told me it was you who talked her into telling me the truth.''

''Don't thank me. I'm sure Sarah would have told you soon in any case. Did she tell you how I convinced her?''

His expression hardened. ''She told me that you think she might be in danger of being arrested.''

''I'm not certain that's the case.'' Mrs. Jeffries hesitated; she wasn't sure how much to tell Taggert. He was still a suspect, albeit a weak one. ''But the possibility did exist.''

''We've got to decide what to do,'' Michael said. ''I'll not have Sarah arrested for a murder she didn't commit.''

Mrs. Jeffries decided to be blunt. ''You may not be able to stop it. Furthermore, as I said, we don't know for certain she is going to be arrested. I'm only making an educated guess. I could be completely wrong.'' She sincerely hoped she was.

''I'll not risk it,'' he said fiercely. ''I'll not risk losing her now and I'll not risk our daughter losing her mother.''

Mrs. Jeffries saw the anguish on his face. ''Inspector Witherspoon is a good man,'' she said gently. ''He won't pursue a case against someone unless he has evidence.''

''But there isn't any evidence against Sarah,'' Michael cried. ''Not any real evidence anyway. She couldn't hurt anyone.''

''And what about you, Mr. Taggert?'' Mrs. Jeffries regarded him steadily.

"Michael couldn't kill anyone, either," Sarah declared softly. She walked to the table. "Neither of us could."

"And I won't let either of us be arrested for a crime we didn't commit," he said, getting to his feet. "We can leave. We don't have to go to the Gilded Lily tonight. We don't have to sit there like sheep being led to the slaughter."

"No, Michael, we're not going to leave," Sarah replied. She came around the table and stood next to him. "We're going to face this and we're going to see it through. I've faith that justice will prevail. We weren't the only ones that hated Haydon."

He grabbed her by the shoulders and pulled her closer. "But what if you are arrested?"

"Then I'll stand trial," she said simply, her eyes never leaving his face. "And if that happens, you'll take care of our daughter."

They stared at one another for a long moment, oblivious to their audience. Michael closed his eyes briefly, as though he was fighting an inner battle with himself. "All right. But if it happens, I'm going to hire you the best counsel money can buy."

Sarah smiled weakly. "Let's not think about that just yet. Besides, Moira will help me if it comes to it."

"No. I'll pay for it."

"Oh Michael—"

"I've got money, Sarah," Michael interrupted. "Lots of it. I inherited a fortune several months ago. Enough to keep us for the rest of our lives. That's why I suggested you and Amanda come away with me. We could take the night train to the continent, catch a ship at one of the French ports; no one would ever find us."

She lifted her chin stubbornly. "I won't hide. I feel like I've been hiding since the day my daughter was born. No. We stay here, regardless of what happens."

"All right, my love." He pulled her closer. "We won't run, but I will take care of both of you, come what may."

Sarah looked at him curiously. "You never said anything about having money . . . and you took that awful job etching those stupid windows for Haydon. Why?"

"I was going to tell you, honestly I was." He gave an embarrassed laugh. "But I was afraid that if Haydon found out I wasn't flat broke, he'd never pay me. I only took that wretched job at the pub so I could see you. Didn't you realize? Haydon did, that's why he was such a bast—" He broke off and flushed as he realized what he'd almost said. "Forgive me, darling. I'll never use that word in your presence again. But we must marry straightaway. No one is ever going to call our child that foul name."

This was all very touching and Mrs. Jeffries would have loved to have sat there all afternoon. It was better than one of the serialized novels in *The Illustrated London News*, but time was wasting.

"Excuse me." She cleared her throat loudly to get their attention. "But we really must move along here."

Sarah broke away and took her seat at the table. Michael sat down as well. "What do you want us to do?" he asked.

"What time are you due at the Gilded Lily?"

"Eight o'clock," Michael replied. "That inspector of yours came around right after I got your note this morning. He insists I be there tonight."

"Moira and I both have to be there as well," Sarah added.

"What exactly did he say?" She directed her question to Michael.

"He said that he had important information about Haydon's murder, but he couldn't tell me what it was." Michael shrugged. "He said he had to show me."

"That's what Moira said he told her," Sarah said excitedly. "Do you think he's found something? Something which will show up the real killer?"

Mrs. Jeffries didn't think he'd found anything. But she wasn't certain. That was what was so impossible about this situation, she didn't know a ruddy thing! "I don't know. But whatever he's up to, I think you both must be there."

"I think we can go in now," Constable Barnes whispered to Inspector Witherspoon. "I just saw Tom and Joanne Dapeers go inside and they're the last ones to arrive."

Witherspoon nodded. He and Barnes were standing in a darkened shop window directly across from the Gilded Lily. A full moon had risen, casting a ghostly light over the quiet street. Witherspoon checked his watch, knowing that he had to time everything perfectly. He was so nervous he was afraid he'd get a headache. On top of that, butterflies were dancing in his stomach, perspiration trickled down his back and his heart was beating so loudly he was sure the constable must hear it. "Are both Molly and Mick inside?" he asked for third time.

Barnes, a patient man, nodded. "Yes. Molly grumbled a bit; she didn't want to come back here. Mick's been inside for over an hour now; he was the first one to arrive."

"Good." Witherspoon took a deep, calming breath, closed his eyes and listened for his inner voice. But he heard nothing. Drat, he thought, this is no time to start having doubts. But what if he was wrong? What if he made a complete fool of himself tonight? He gave himself a shake. There was no point in worrying about that now: the die was cast. Everyone was in position. Visions of the records room swam in his head, and for once Witherspoon didn't find the image soothing.

"Er, sir?" Barnes prodded. "Are you all right?"

"Perfectly, Constable. Thank you for inquiring. Right,

then, let's get this done with. We've a killer to catch to-night, Barnes. Justice must be served.''

The inspector boldly started across Minyard Street with Barnes right on his heels. Their footsteps echoed loudly on the stone pavement. Witherspoon noticed the night had become eerily silent. The foot traffic had disappeared, and except for the clip-clop of the occasional hansom, the street was deserted.

Bright light spilled out the front windows of the pub. Witherspoon grasped the door handle, gave it a turn, steeled himself and the two men stepped inside.

As instructed, Molly and Mick were behind the bar. Mick was polishing glasses with a white tea towel. Molly was standing with her arms folded across her chest and a disgruntled expression on her face.

The inspector glanced quickly around the room. No one looked particularly happy to be there. Moira Dapeers and her sister-in-law were sitting to the left of the bar, talking quietly. Michael Taggert was standing alone in front of the partition leading to the saloon bar. Tom and Joanne Dapeers were sitting at one of the round tables. Tom was drumming his fingers against the wood and Joanne appeared to be glaring at a gas lamp on the far wall. Her head snapped around at the sound of the door banging shut.

''It's about time you got here,'' she snapped. ''We've been waiting for a good half hour.''

That was an exaggeration, but Witherspoon was far too polite to contradict a lady. ''My apologies, madam. I didn't mean to keep any of you waiting. Unfortunately, I was unavoidably detained at the Yard.''

''What's this all about?'' Tom Dapeers asked. ''We've got a business to run, you know. Can't hang about here all night.''

''And I've got a missionary society meeting,'' Moira Dapeers added. "I don't like to be late. It upsets the reverend dreadfully."

"Anyone want a beer?" Molly interrupted. When no one answered her, she shrugged and helped herself.

Michael Taggert said nothing.

Witherspoon walked into the center of the room. Barnes moved to the far side of the bar and whipped out his notebook.

"First of all, I'd like to thank all of you for coming," he began.

"We didn't have much choice," Molly muttered loudly enough for the whole room to hear.

The inspector ignored her. "I know you've all been dreadfully inconvenienced, but I assure you, your presence tonight is most important. Most important, indeed."

"Wiggins," Hatchet whispered urgently, "will you kindly get your elbow out of my ribs? It's rather painful."

"Sorry," Wiggins hissed. "But it's hard to see through all these ruddy lines on the glass."

"They're called etchings," Hatchet corrected. "And we really must take care not to be seen. Besides, you're supposed to be keeping a lookout. It wouldn't do for a police constable to spot us and ask what we're doing."

"We ain't doin' nothin' but lookin' in the window of a public 'ouse," Wiggins replied. He wondered why he always got stuck doing the borin' bits like keepin' watch.

"A closed public house," Hatchet pointed out. "And we did promise Mrs. Jeffries we'd make sure the inspector didn't see us." As Hatchet and Wiggins had had to argue for a good hour even to get the others to agree that their coming along to the Gilded Lily to keep an eye on things might be a good idea, Hatchet was determined not to get caught in any embarrassing situations. He wouldn't have liked to explain to Inspector Witherspoon what he and Wiggins were doing out here.

"Oh, all right," Wiggins muttered reluctantly. "I'll keep watch." He dragged his gaze away from the window and dutifully glanced up and down the street. "But I don't see why. No one's goin' to be botherin' us; we're just standin' 'ere. There's no one about. Least not any police that I can see."

Hatchet was worried about the police they couldn't see. But he didn't want to excite the lad.

"Any sign of Smythe in there?" Wiggins poked Hatchet in the ribs.

"Ouch. Will you kindly cease and desist prodding at my person whenever you speak to me?" he snapped softly. "I'm going to be covered in bruises by the time I get home."

"Sorry. But I wanted to get yer attention," Wiggins apologized. "Do ya see him?"

"Who?"

"Smythe. Is he in there?"

"No, I don't see him." Hatchet craned his neck over the etching of a lily. "At least if he is, he's well out of sight."

"I don't think he's in there," Wiggins said. He squinted as he saw a figure turn the corner and head down Minyard Street in the direction of the pub. "We'da seen the carriage if he was. What's goin' on in there now?"

"Very little," Hatchet replied. "The inspector is standing in the center of the room, talking. The others are just sitting there, watching him."

"What's he sayin'?" Wiggins asked eagerly, taking his eyes off the approaching figure for just a moment and glancing toward the window. "Anythin' excitin'?"

"I can't hear what he's saying with you chattering in my ear, can I?" Hatchet cocked his ear toward the glass. He could hear the inspector's voice, but he couldn't quite make out the words.

Wiggins tugged on Hatchet's sleeve again, taking care not to poke his person anywhere. "Uh, Hatchet, I think we'd best get a move on."

"Shh." Hatchet silenced him. "I think I can hear what he's saying."

Wiggins saw that the figure was definitely a man, a man wearing a police helmet. "Uh, Hatchet." He poked him directly in the ribs again. "Get away from that window."

"Will you please be quiet?" the butler snapped. "I'm trying to hear what the inspector's saying . . ."

"Hatchet," Wiggins hissed frantically, "listen to me. There's a copper coming and he's headed right this way."

"As you are all aware, Mr. Haydon Dapeers was recently murdered in this very pub," Witherspoon said. "He walked through that hallway"—he pointed to the hall beyond the bar—"into the taproom at the end and never came back."

"Yes, Inspector," Moira Dapeers said dryly, "we do know that. But what's that got to do with us being here tonight?"

Witherspoon smiled politely. He could feel beads of sweat running down his neck. He hoped they weren't too noticeable. "Actually, madam, it has quite a bite to do with your all being asked to come here tonight. This investigation has been most difficult, most difficult, indeed. The back door of the pub was probably locked that night and there was a street brawl going on just outside on the street. Most of you claim you were outside watching that brawl when Mr. Dapeers was killed. So what I thought I'd have you do—" He broke off as the front door opened and Constable Griffith rushed inside.

"Sorry to interrupt you, sir," Griffith said respectfully. "But we've got a bit of a situation."

Annoyed, the inspector frowned. "I'm rather busy here, Constable," he complained. "Can't it wait?"

Griffith shook his head. "No, sir, it can't. We've had a bit of a break on that stabbin' victim we pulled out of the Thames yesterday."

"Someone's confessed?" Witherspoon asked eagerly.

"No, sir." Griffith grinned. "But we've got us a witness. An eyewitness who saw the whole thing."

"For goodness' sakes, why didn't he come forward before this?" Witherspoon cried impatiently. "That poor woman's been dead for several days."

Griffith shrugged. "He's a petty crook, sir. Doesn't much like the police. He sent us a note, sir. Seems he's had dealings with you before and you're the only one he trusts."

Witherspoon sighed dramatically. "I suppose you want me to go along to the Yard now and take this fellow's statement."

"No, sir," Griffith said quickly. "He won't set foot in a police station. He wants to meet you at the spot where we found the body. He claims that's where the killin' took place. I reckon it's worth our while, sir. He says he saw the whole thing."

"Do you have a name for this person, Constable?"

"No, sir. But he knows you, sir. Wants you to be there at ten o'clock."

"Ten o'clock?" Witherspoon pulled out his watch and checked the time. "Gracious, I can't possibly do that. It's going to take at least that long to finish here and then I wanted to stop and have a bite to eat. I haven't had anything all day and I'm rather hungry."

"We won't have time to finish here, sir," Barnes interjected. "I reckon we'd best just call it a night, sir. I'm not sure this was goin' to work anyway."

"Inspector Witherspoon." Joanne Dapeers rose to her feet. "My husband and I have a business to run. Obviously, you're going to be busy this evening. I've no idea why you dragged us down here and I've no idea what you hoped to accomplish, but if you don't mind, I'd like to leave."

"I would too," Moira Dapeers echoed. "Coming here has been most inconvenient."

"In that case, madam," Witherspoon said, "you can leave. As a matter of fact, you can all go. I'm so sorry to have troubled you. I'll contact everyone tomorrow."

"Now, just a minute," Michael Taggert yelled. "You didn't even tell us what you wanted. Why you had us come here."

"Sorry, Mr. Taggert, I'll explain everything tomorrow." He nodded at Barnes and started for the front door. "Come along, Barnes. If we hurry, we can have a bite to eat before we meet this witness."

"I knew we should have gone with them," Luty Belle cried. "It's almost ten o'clock and they ain't back yet."

"Now, Luty, calm yourself," Mrs. Jeffries said soothingly. "I'm sure Hatchet and Wiggins are just fine."

Betsy snorted. "Of course they're fine, they're out and about and in the thick of it. We're stuck here in this ruddy house." As she'd wanted to go with the men, she was most put out to be sitting in the kitchen of Upper Edmonton Gardens watching the clock.

"I hate waiting," Mrs. Goodge said. "Makes me all nervous like. I wonder what's happening tonight? Do you think the inspector has caught the killer?"

"Perhaps." Mrs. Jeffries didn't think the inspector had caught anything except a bad case of ruining his career, but she didn't want to infect the others with her dismal view of the situation. She sighed inwardly. By tomorrow, it would all be over. The inspector's career would be in shreds and years of boredom loomed in front of her. Witherspoon would be back in the records room and the household would be doing nothing but polishing, cleaning and cooking. There wouldn't be any more interesting murders to solve, no more dashing about London searching for clues and following suspects. No more adventures.

"Buck up, Hepzibah," Luty ordered. "It ain't over yet. The inspector might know exactly what he's doin'. He might surprise us all and actually catch this killer."

Mrs. Jeffries smiled glumly but said nothing. There was no use in trying to keep everyone's spirits up, she wasn't doing a very good job of keeping her own up.

"Without our help?" Betsy laughed harshly. "Not likely. He don't know half of what we know about this case. He doesn't know about McNally, he doesn't know about Moira Dapeers carryin' on with that reverend—"

"And I don't think he knows about Dapeers havin' that disease, either," Mrs. Goodge put in.

"Maybe he knows something we don't know," Luty argued. "Maybe we ain't as smart as we think we are."

"Oh Luty," Mrs. Jeffries said. "We're not saying the inspector isn't intelligent. He is a perfectly capable policeman. We're only saying there's too much about this murder that he doesn't know."

"And I'm sayin' we don't know what he knows!" Luty cried passionately. "Has it occurred to any of you that the inspector may have important clues that we don't? Just because we think we know more than he does don't make it true. He ain't been sittin' around here twiddlin' his thumbs for the past few days. He's been out investigatin'."

Mrs. Jeffries stared at her for a long moment and then smiled slowly. "You know, Luty, I stand corrected. You're absolutely right. We don't know what he knows. Perhaps

Inspector Witherspoon will solve this murder.''

"Well," Betsy said, "much as I'd hate to think he could do it without our help, at least if he does catch the killer, it'll keep him out of the records room."

"And it'll keep us doin' our own detecting," Mrs. Goodge added brightly.

The moonlight reflecting off the Thames cast the deserted dock in a faint glow of light. The lone man stood at the end of the pier, staring out onto the river. He hadn't brought a lamp with him; with the full moon overhead, there was no need. He leaned negligently against the old wood of the piling, his eyes straight ahead on the river.

A figure watched him. It stood quietly in the shadowed doorway of the empty warehouse at the other end of the pier. Wearing a long, dark cloak that blended into the darkness, the intruder stepped forward and looked around, making certain there was no one about. But the place was deserted, empty. There wouldn't be any witnesses to this.

Slowly, carefully, the cloaked figure moved away from the safety of the darkness and stepped out onto the pier. One of the wooden planks groaned and the intruder stopped and stared at the man standing at the end.

The man didn't move, didn't turn to look about and see if he was still alone.

The killer smiled and grasped the knife tighter.

This had better be fast and hard. The man looked pretty big. Best to avoid a struggle. The figure started quickly down the dock, stepping softly, wanting the attack to be a surprise. The planks groaned slightly, but the man must have been deep in his thoughts, for he didn't seem to hear.

He didn't turn and look. Stupid fool.

The knife came out from beneath the cloak, its long blade

gleaming in the moonlight. Quickly now, before he spots
me.

The footsteps began to move faster, faster. A nervous
hand raised the knife in the air. One stab right through the
back and it would all be over. No one would ever know
the truth.

The victim was only a few feet away now, just a few
more feet.

Just at that moment the man turned.

"Halt," a voice cried in the night.

There was a shrill blast of a police whistle and the sound
of pounding footsteps. The murderer turned to see half a
dozen policemen running at full speed down the pier. The
figure lunged at the man, the knife slashing through the air.

"Bloody 'ell," the man yelled. He ducked to one side,
threw his arm out and grabbed at the cloak.

The killer stumbled and fell, dropping the knife. The man
kicked the knife to one side. The figure, on its knees and
hampered by the heavy cloak, lunged toward the shiny
blade but, before reaching it, was grabbed by the man and
held in place.

They struggled silently in the night.

Suddenly they were surrounded by a half-dozen men.

Lamps were lighted and a worried voice cried, "Smythe,
Smythe, are you all right? Speak to me, man, speak to me."

"I'm fine, Inspector." Smythe got off the struggling,
cloaked body and moved to one side. The figure went perfectly still.

"Thank God," Witherspoon said. "I'd never forgive
myself if you were hurt."

"Not to worry, sir," he said, his attention focused on
the person who'd just tried to shove a knife in his back.
"There's no 'arm done. I 'eard 'im comin' and was ready.
I'm just a bit dirty from rollin' on the pier."

Witherspoon stepped toward the huddled, cloaked figure. Barnes was right beside him, holding a lamp up. "Please get up," the inspector ordered.

It didn't move. Witherspoon thought about repeating himself, but then decided he'd look rather foolish talking to a lumpy mass that refused to respond. He was so relieved his plan had worked that he was feeling rather light-headed. Gracious, for a moment back there he'd been frightened his trap was a bit of a wash. In truth, when he'd come up with this plan, he'd been sure it would lure the killer out into the open. But as the minutes had ticked by and no one had come, he'd grown very worried. Very worried, indeed. But then they'd spotted the cloaked figure stealing onto the dock. He'd known then that his trap would work. But he'd had a bad moment or two. Especially when Smythe had persisted in standing there like a sacrificial lamb. Why, it had almost given him heart failure when he'd seen that knife.

"Er, sir," Barnes said gently, "don't you want to see who it is?"

Witherspoon started. "Of course." He leaned over, grasped the hood of the cloak and tossed it back, revealing the face of the killer. They stared at one another for a long moment.

Finally, the inspector said, "Joanne Dapeers, you're under arrest for the murders of Ellen Hoxton and Haydon Dapeers."

CHAPTER 11

"There was really nothing we could do to salvage the situation," Hatchet explained earnestly. "Once the constable came on the scene, we'd no choice but to leave." He shrugged helplessly. "When the coast was clear again, so to speak, the inspector had gone."

"Well, fiddlesticks," Luty cried in disgust. "So we're no better off than if you two hadn't even a-bothered to go! We still don't know what the inspector's got up to tonight."

"I told you I should have gone with them," Betsy muttered. "I'da kept my eye on the front door instead of scarpering off like some thief in the night."

"It weren't our fault," Wiggins argued. "That police constable come straight for us. We 'ad to leave; you told us to make sure the inspector didn't catch sight of us."

"Couldn't you have just crossed the road and pretended you was out taking an evening constitutional?" Mrs. Goodge suggested sarcastically.

"No, madam," Hatchet replied stiffly. "We couldn't.

What young Wiggins has failed to mention, but is quite pertinent to the circumstances, is that the constable coming down Minyard Street wasn't the only constable in the vicinity. There were two constables on patrol on Bonham Road when we dashed around the corner. Furthermore, we both had the distinct impression they were keeping a sharp eye on us. It was impossible to do anything but carry on and get out of there. Mrs. Jeffries had made it quite clear that it would be disastrous if the inspector had any idea we were even in the area.''

''You both did very well,'' Mrs. Jeffries said quickly. ''Very well, indeed.''

''But they didn't learn nothing!'' Mrs. Goodge snapped. ''We still don't know what was going on tonight.''

''Useless as teats on a bull,'' Luty murmured.

''I'da done something,'' Betsy promised. ''I wouldn't have come back with nothing.''

Mrs. Jeffries frowned at the women. ''Really, you're being most unfair. Hatchet and Wiggins did precisely as we asked them to do. It's hardly their fault that they were unable to complete their assignment. Besides, we do know more than we did earlier. Thanks to these two''—she smiled at the men—''we know exactly which group of suspects the inspector thinks are suspects.''

''That's right,'' Wiggins agreed eagerly. ''You wouldn'a knowed who was in that pub tonight unless we'd gone there. Now we know it's got to be one of them that the inspector thinks is the killer.''

''What about Smythe?'' Betsy asked. She hadn't wanted to bring him up, but the truth was she was getting worried. ''You said you didn't see him tonight. What's he up to, then?''

Just at that moment Fred leapt up from his perch under Wiggins's chair. He cocked his head for a moment, listening. Then he ran for the back door just as they all heard the sound of the carriage pulling up.

"That must be the inspector," Mrs. Jeffries warned. She glanced at Luty and Hatchet, wondering how she would explain their presence in the kitchen at half-past eleven at night.

Luty grinned mischievously. "Don't worry, Hepzibah, I'll handle the inspector."

A moment later they heard the back door open and close. From the hallway, they heard Witherspoon greet his friend. "Good dog," he said brightly. He continued to talk to the animal as he walked down the hall, not realizing that he had a kitchen full of people listening to his every word. "You waited up for me. What a loyal fellow you are. Come on, now let's go to the kitchen and scrounge up a cup of tea. Maybe if we're very lucky—" He came into the brightly lighted kitchen and blinked. His entire household, as well as Luty Belle Crookshank and her butler, Hatchet, were sitting at the kitchen table drinking tea. "Gracious, this is a surprise."

"Evenin', Inspector," Luty greeted him enthusiastically.

"Good evening, Mrs. Crookshank." He looked at Mrs. Jeffries, wondering what on earth was going on. "It's very nice to see you."

Hatchet bowed formally in the inspector's direction. "Good evening, sir. I trust you're well."

"Quite well, thank you." As the inspector couldn't think of what to do, he sat down at the table.

"I expect you're wondering why we're here," Luty said conversationally.

"Well, er . . . you know it's always delightful to see you," he began.

Luty interrupted him with a laugh. "Oh don't be so modest, Inspector. You know danged good and well why we're here.''

''I do?''

''Now don't be so coy.'' She smiled broadly. ''You know what an admirer of yours I am.''

Witherspoon flushed in pleasure. ''That's most kind of you to say, but really, I'm only a simple public servant.''

Luty waved her hand dismissively. ''Nonsense. You're the most brilliant detective on either side of the Atlantic and that's a fact. 'Corse, once I wormed it out of Hepzibah that you was fixin' to catch the murderer of that publican tonight, that you had ya a foolproof plan, wild horses couldn'a kept me away.'' She leaned toward him eagerly. ''Now don't be annoyed with the household, Inspector, it ain't their fault me and Hatchet barged in on the off chance we'd get to see ya. It's my fault. They're just bein' polite. And they was all concerned about ya too, wantin' to make sure you was all right. Police work is so dangerous! They all know how brave ya are, how you'll throw yerself into the thick of things without worryin' about yer own hide.''

Mrs. Jeffries raised an eyebrow and glanced at Hatchet. He rolled his eyes heavenward. Luty was laying it on thicker than custard, and by the pleased expression on the inspector's face, he believed every word of it.

Witherspoon smiled broadly. ''I wouldn't dream of getting angry at my staff. Their devotion to me is most touching.''

''Excuse me, sir,'' Betsy said. ''But is Smythe all right?''

''He's just fine. He's taking the carriage to the livery. Smythe was very brave tonight. Very brave, indeed. Actually, it's a bit nice to come home and find everyone waiting for me. So much better than walking into a dark, empty house. I say, are those Mrs. Goodge's wonderful sausage rolls I see?'' He pointed to the plate in the center of the table.

"Let me serve you, sir," the cook said quickly, grabbing an empty plate and forking three of the delicacies onto it.

"I'll pour you some tea," Mrs. Jeffries offered.

"Excellent. I'm positively famished." He smiled broadly at Luty. "As Mrs. Crookshank has gone to all the trouble of being here tonight, perhaps I'd better tell you what happened." He stopped and stuffed a bite of the roll in his mouth.

They all waited impatiently. But the air of tension in the kitchen had gone. He didn't act like a man who'd just ruined his career.

"Let me see," Witherspoon mumbled around his second mouthful of food, "where should I begin? Ah, I know. I caught the killer. My plan worked."

Mrs. Jeffries sighed silently in relief. Betsy and Mrs. Goodge exchanged glances, as though they couldn't believe what they'd just heard. Wiggins said nothing; he just stared at the inspector with a look of awe on his face.

"Naturally, you caught him," Luty exclaimed. "Now, tell us all the details."

"It wasn't a him," the inspector replied. "It was a her."

"A her?" Mrs. Jeffries asked. She crossed her fingers in her lap, hoping that it wasn't Sarah Hewett.

Witherspoon nodded and took a quick gulp of tea. "Indeed. Of course, once I realized why Haydon Dapeers had been killed in the first place, it was simple to determine who the killer actually was, you see. Mind you, I didn't understand what the motive was until I spoke to the gentlemen from Bestal's Brewery. Then, of course, everything fell into place."

Mrs. Jeffries didn't quite understand. From the expressions on the faces of the others, she was fairly certain they didn't have a clue about what he was on about either. "I'm afraid I don't understand."

"It's really quite simple," he replied airily. "Of course, I wasn't sure which one of them it was. Then I remembered what she was wearing the night of the murder. Struck me as odd, even then. It was the parasol and the muff, you see. Far too ornate for a quick trip to the pub, wouldn't you say?" He helped himself to another sausage roll. "I've learned to pay attention to what people are wearing when a murder has been committed. That dreadful business at the Jubilee Ball last summer taught me that."

Everyone knew that Witherspoon was referring to a rather difficult case they'd helped solve the previous year, but knowing he was referring to that old murder didn't help. They were still confused, but no one wanted to interrupt him.

Except Luty. "Hold on a minute, Inspector," she demanded. "My old brain don't work as fast as yours. I'm not following you."

"Sorry," he apologized. "I am going a bit fast. Let me start at the beginning."

"We'd be most grateful if you did, sir," Mrs. Jeffries interjected.

"Let me see now, how best to start," he murmured. "I suppose I ought to tell you about my trip to Bestal's the day after the murder. Yes, that's probably what I ought to do."

Mrs. Jeffries thought he ought to tell them who he'd arrested, but before she could make that reasonable suggestion, he was off again.

"It was what Mr. Magil and Mr. Pump told me that put me on the right trail," he continued. "You see, Haydon Dapeers had written them a letter. That's why they'd gone to the Gilded Lily the night of the murder, you see. They wanted him to name names.''

''Name names?'' Wiggins repeated.

''Right. Dapeers claimed that someone was watering down their beer.''

''Watering down their beer?'' Wiggins was beginning to sound like a parrot.

''I don't understand,'' Mrs. Jeffries said; she fought to keep her voice calm.

''Of course you don't,'' Witherspoon exclaimed. ''And neither did I until they explained it. You see, many breweries loan money to publicans to buy pubs. They do that on the condition that the pub will sell their beer exclusively. Haydon Dapeers had written and told them that one of the publicans Bestal's had loaned money to was watering down their beer. Bestal's doesn't like that. None of the breweries do. As a matter of fact, if they catch a publican doing it, they call the loan.'' He leaned back and smiled. ''As soon as I heard that, I was fairly certain who had the strongest reason for wanting Dapeers dead. Of course, proving it was a bit of a challenge. But we came up with something in the end.''

''You mean, sir,'' Mrs. Goodge asked, ''the motive for this murder was watered beer?''

He nodded enthusiastically. ''Precisely.''

They exchanged glances around the table. Mrs. Jeffries couldn't believe it. All their investigating, all their dashing about and talking to everyone under the sun. All of the time and effort and digging up clues and none of them had even come close to the right motive for Haydon Dapeers's death. James McNally and his gambling debt, Moira Dapeers and her love of the Reverend Ballantine, Sarah Hewett and her desperation to keep Haydon quiet about her daughter, none of it had mattered. She felt like an utter failure. By the stunned expressions on the faces of the others, she thought they probably felt the same way.

"Of course, once I realized what the motive was, knowing who killed him was easy," Witherspoon continued. "As I said, it was proving it that was going to be difficult. Then, of course, Ellen Hoxton's body turned up in the Thames and I knew for certain I was on the right track. That's when I set my trap."

"Who's Ellen Hoxton?" Luty demanded.

"She was a barmaid at the Black Horse," the inspector explained. "And she knew that the Black Horse was watering their beer. That's why she was murdered, you see."

Mrs. Jeffries had had enough. Their dear inspector was enjoying himself far too much; if they let him witter on like this, they'd be here until breakfast. "No, sir, we don't see anything. First of all, who did you arrest tonight?"

"Gracious, didn't I mention that?"

"No," they all cried in unison.

He blinked. "Oh, sorry. I meant to tell you. It was Joanne Dapeers. That's who the killer was. She murdered both Ellen Hoxton and Haydon Dapeers. She killed Ellen first, though. She'd sacked Ellen for talking back to her. Ellen, in turn, threatened to tell everyone that Joanne Dapeers was watering the beer at the Black Horse and their other two pubs. Joanne knew that their loans would be called if Bestal's found out what they were up to, so she stabbed Ellen. But she made a mistake: Ellen Hoxton had already told Haydon Dapeers what was going on. He paid her for the information." He shook his head in disgust. "Five pounds—he gave that poor woman five pounds and it cost her her life."

"How dreadful," Mrs. Goodge muttered.

"Go on, sir," Mrs. Jeffries urged, "tell us the rest of it. How did you figure all this out?"

"To be perfectly honest, I didn't understand for a couple of days. I was fairly certain that it was either Tom or Joanne Dapeers who'd done the killings, but it wasn't until I remembered what Joanne was wearing on the night of Haydon's murder that I was sure that she was the actual killer. It could have been either of them, you see. The killer had brought the weapon to the Gilded Lily. Molly, the barmaid, verified that the knives in the kitchen of the Lily were still in the drawer, so I knew that the murderer had to have brought the murder weapon."

"I don't follow you, sir," Mrs. Jeffries said.

"The knife had a ten-inch blade," he explained. "It would be very difficult for a man to carry a knife of that size in his coat or trouser pockets; he'd be in danger of cutting himself quite badly. No one walked in that night with any parcels or packages on their person and the other women all had on light summer frocks and no parasols. Joanne Dapeers had on a brilliant red dress and carried both a parasol and a huge, matching muff. When I remembered that, I knew it had to be her."

"She brought the knife in the muff," Mrs. Jeffries said thoughtfully. She was impressed with the inspector's reasoning. "She'd planned on killing him."

"Precisely." Witherspoon beamed. "She'd already killed once."

"Ellen Hoxton," Betsy said, "to keep her quiet about the watered beer."

"Right." The inspector reached for his tea. "Poor Ellen Hoxton. I think that she was probably foolish enough to tell Joanne what she'd done. From what the barman at the Black Horse told me, Ellen was quite hot-tempered and bold. Joanne knew she had to do something, she knew that Haydon wouldn't hesitate to go straight to the brewery. If that happened, they'd lose the loans on all three of their pubs and they'd be ruined. I think she planned on killing him that night, but when she walked in and saw that Pump and Magil were already there, she decided to do it quickly. Luckily for her, the brawl broke out just as Haydon went into the taproom. She slipped down the hall, coshed him on the head with her parasol to stun him, shoved the knife in his back and screamed her head off for help. Clever, really, and quite daring. She almost got away with it too." He picked up his cup and drained the last of his tea. "I'm quite tired," he announced with a yawn. "If you don't mind, I think I'll go to bed now."

Several of them opened their mouths to protest, but Mrs. Jeffries silenced them with a look. "Of course, sir. You must be dreadfully tired."

Witherspoon rose, said good night and left the kitchen. As soon as he was out of earshot, they all started talking at once.

"He didn't tell us the half of it," Luty complained.

"What was this plan of 'is, then?" Wiggins muttered.

"Why was everyone at the pub tonight?" Hatchet asked.

"What's this about Smythe bein' brave?" Betsy demanded. "Where is he anyway? He should be home by now."

Mrs. Jeffries raised a hand for silence. "We'll find out the rest from Smythe. He should be home anytime now. It's no good badgering the inspector when he's tired; he'll only get us all confused."

But Smythe didn't show up for another half hour. When he walked in, whistling as he came down the back hall, Betsy was pacing the kitchen. Luty was glaring at the clock, Hatchet was drumming his fingers on the tabletop and Mrs. Goodge was clearing the table. Wiggins was asleep.

"Where've you been?" Betsy demanded the moment he stepped into the kitchen.

"Good evenin', all." He gave them a wide grin. "I've been seein' to the 'orses. They 'ad quite a run today, they did."

"And what's this about you bein' so bloomin' brave?" Betsy snapped. "What've you been up to?"

"Do sit down, Smythe," Mrs. Jeffries invited. "The inspector has told us some of what happened, but not all of it."

"But make it quick," Luty ordered. "It's gettin' late." She reached over and poked Wiggins in the ribs. "Wake up if you want to hear what happened."

Wiggins jerked awake and looked around in confusion.

Smythe sat down at the table. "Did he tell you it was Joanne Dapeers?"

"Yes," Mrs. Jeffries said, "and he told us how he'd figured out she was the killer, but he didn't say a word about how he trapped her."

Smythe grinned. "It worked too, I was sure 'e were fixin' to ruin 'is career." He told the others how he'd driven the inspector all over London that day. "We stopped at Bestal's and the inspector was in talkin' to 'em a long time. He told me later he were confirmin' that all three of Tom and Joanne's pubs were bought on loans from the Bestal's and that they still owed a pretty penny for all of 'em. After that, he made me drive him to Scotland Yard. I dawdled all I could, but we finally got there. When we pulled up, the inspector asked me to come inside. Scared the life out of me, it did. Him standin' in front of the chief inspector and talkin' about this daft plan of 'is."

"What plan?" Mrs. Goodge asked querulously. She was tired, sleepy and getting crankier by the minute.

"I'm comin' to that," Smythe said. "It were a good plan, actually. But at the time I thought it was daft. You see, no one knew that Ellen Hoxton's body 'ad been found.

The inspector got everyone together at the Lily that night because he was goin' to trick the killer. 'E fixed it so Constable Griffith would pop in and tell the inspector that there was an eyewitness to the Hoxton murder, but it were a petty crook who wouldn't come into a police station to talk and 'e'd only talk to Witherspoon. Griffith was told to make sure he said the inspector was to meet this crook at the spot where Ellen's body was found. She'd been pulled out of the Thames with a stab wound in her back, just like Haydon Dapeers.''

"Then why didn't her body float off?" Wiggins asked.

" 'Cause her dress got caught on a piling,'' Smythe replied. "Anyway, the inspector reasoned that only the killer would know where Ellen's murder took place. So he played like 'e was right irritated and told Griffith 'e'd meet this witness. Griffith made a point of sayin' that the man would be waitin' for him at ten o'clock.'' Smythe laughed. "The inspector did that on purpose too. He wanted to give the murderer a chance to get there first and try to kill the witness. You'da been proud of him, playactin' with the best of 'em.''

"And who was this man?" Betsy asked archly. "This witness.''

Smythe shifted in his chair and glanced down at the table. "Well, uh, they was goin' to use a police constable, but the chief inspector was afraid that wouldn't look right when the case got to court.'' He stopped and cleared his throat. "So the inspector asked me to 'ave a go at it.''

Betsy's eyes narrowed. "So you was standing there waitin' for this crazy woman to slip up and shove a knife in your back.''

"Now, it wasn't like that, lass,'' he soothed. "There were police all over the dock.'' Smythe thought it best not to go into any more details about what had really happened on the pier. "They nabbed her before she got close to me."

"So his plan worked," Mrs. Jeffries said thoughtfully.

"Worked all right, they caught her red-handed. Joanne Dapeers killed two people. She's goin' to 'ang."

The next morning, the household waited until after Witherspoon had left for the day before gathering around the kitchen table.

"We've spent most of this bloomin' case around this table," Wiggins complained. "Might as well 'ave not even bothered tryin' to do any investigatin' at all. Fat lot of good it did us."

"Now, Wiggins," Mrs. Jeffries said soothingly. "We did the best we could." She was as disgusted as the rest of them, but she certainly didn't want it to show. They mustn't be petty. Occasionally, the inspector was going to solve a case on his own.

"Wiggins is right," Betsy grumbled. "We shouldn'a bothered. All that running around I did, following that silly McNally, talking my way into that missionary society, going to that stupid pub with Hamilton. None of it had a thing to do with the murder. Not a ruddy thing."

"Think how I feel?" Mrs. Goodge cried. "I had my sources out sussing up nonsense on a dead publican. My reputation's in shreds, it is."

Smythe shrugged. "We was tryin' to 'elp, so we shouldn't feel too bad about it."

"You're only sayin' that because you was in on it at the end," Betsy said accusingly. She was sure there was a lot he wasn't telling them about the previous night's activities.

"This is pointless," Mrs. Jeffries said bluntly. "We're all sitting around here with long faces and grumbling because we're annoyed the inspector solved the crime on his own."

"Maybe we ain't as clever as we thought we were," Wiggins suggested morosely. "We didn't even come close to figurin' out this one."

As Mrs. Jeffries and the others were well aware of that fact, they didn't find the footman's statement particularly helpful. "We would have figured it out eventually."

"Do you really think so?" Wiggins asked, looking hopeful.

"Of course." Mrs. Jeffries forced herself to smile. "There will be other cases."

"I think we've lost our touch," Betsy said. "I don't think we'll ever solve another murder again."

"He'll hog them all," Mrs. Goodge announced darkly. "He's got a taste for it now that's he gotten lucky—"

"Lucky?" Mrs. Jeffries interrupted. "Really, Mrs. Goodge, I'm as upset as you are about our failure on this case, but I hardly think it's fair to say the inspector got 'lucky.' He solved this case with logic and reason."

"And listenin' to his inner voice," Wiggins interjected rudely. "If it 'adn't been for that bloomin' inner voice, we'da 'ad a decent crack at the case."

"Honestly, you're all impossible today." Mrs. Jeffries rose to her feet. "We'll talk about this later, when you've all had a chance to calm down."

She left them to their misery and went upstairs. She was as worried as the rest of them. Despite their grumbling about inner voices and hogging cases, she knew what was really bothering everyone. It bothered her too. They'd been so wrong about this case. So very wrong. None of them had even come close to determining the motive or the killer. As Betsy had said, maybe they'd lost their touch.

Mrs. Jeffries went up to her sitting room and pulled a volume of Mr. Walt Whitman from her shelves. But she couldn't concentrate on the beautiful words; they failed to soothe her as they usually did.

For the next few days everyone in the household walked about with long, glum faces. Even a visit from Luty and Hatchet failed to cheer people up: it was difficult to be cheered by visitors as morose as you were.

Witherspoon, ridiculously happy himself, didn't appear to notice his household's mood. Or so Mrs. Jeffries thought until early one evening.

"Will you join me in a sherry?" he suggested as she took his hat and put it on the rack. "There's something I want to talk with you about."

"Certainly, sir." They went into the drawing room and she poured them both a sherry. Taking a seat opposite him, she folded her hands in her lap. "What is it, sir? Is there something amiss in the household?"

"Oh no, Mrs. Jeffries. As always, it runs perfectly." He smiled warmly. "I have you to thank for that."

"There's no need to thank me, sir. I'm only doing my job."

He looked disappointed at her words and she wished she could take them back. Sometimes she forgot what a sensitive soul he was. "I mean, it's what I've been trained to do, sir," she explained quickly. "What I enjoy doing. Now, sir, what did you need to speak to me about?"

"My last case." He took a sip of sherry and put the glass down on the table next to him. "I didn't really enjoy it much."

Surprised, she stared at him. "Really, sir?"

"I'll admit I was glad my plan worked and that we arrested the killer, but I must say, I was very worried." He clasped his hands in front of him. "If I'd been wrong, the consequences could have been most severe. Most severe indeed."

"But you weren't wrong, sir," she reminded him.

"But I could have been." He smiled wryly. "It's all very well listening to one's inner voice, Mrs. Jeffries. But it doesn't make for an interesting case. No, from now on I think I'll go back to my old ways. I know how much you and the others like hearing about my investigations. Gracious, I hadn't realized how dreadfully selfish I'd been till I arrived home that night and found Mrs. Crookshank and Hatchet lying in wait for me. I've been very selfish."

Mrs. Jeffries's spirits soared. Thank goodness he was coming to his senses. "You mean you won't be listening to your inner voice anymore?" she asked.

"Oh, I'll listen to it," he replied. "But I certainly want to discuss my cases with you. You're an excellent sounding board, Mrs. Jeffries."

"That's kind of you, sir."

"I'm not being kind, I'm being truthful." He frowned. "In the end, this case turned out well, but as I said, it could easily have gone the wrong way."

Mrs. Jeffries got to her feet. "I'm glad you feel that way, sir. To be truthful, I did feel a bit left out. You know how much I love hearing about your methods of investigation."

"I promise you," he said earnestly, "the next time you'll hear all about it. I won't be selfish again."

"Thank you." She started for the hall. "If you'll excuse me, I've got to go to the kitchen."

"But you haven't finished your sherry," he called.

"I'll finish it later, sir," she cried gaily. "I've just remembered an urgent matter I must tell the rest of the staff."